An ALIEN

IN THE jam

Factory

CHRISSIE
SAINS

ILLUSTRATED BY
JENNY
TAYLOR

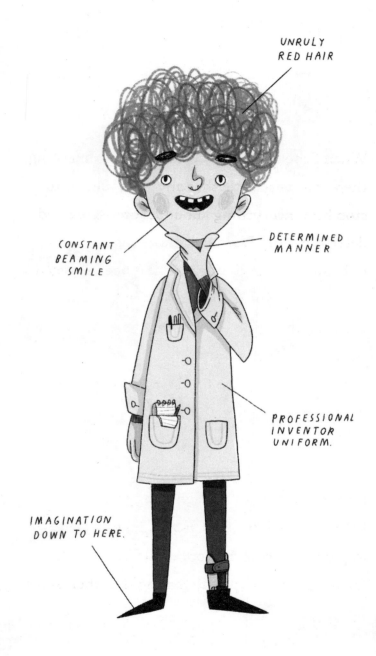

UNRULY
RED HAIR

CONSTANT
BEAMING
SMILE

DETERMINED
MANNER

PROFESSIONAL
INVENTOR
UNIFORM.

IMAGINATION
DOWN TO HERE.

My Newest <u>**JAM**</u> Inventions

Cherry Candy Floss

ELECTRIFYING
elderberry Balls

$x = \frac{3}{8} \cdot \frac{2(3x-1)^4}{4z}$ = formula

Cherry : Candy Floss
3 : 7 *

MELTS IN mouth

Jam slice *
- like a cheese slice, PUT STRaight on sanDWICH

10 cm
10 cm
4.5 mm thick

y
x

pineapple {with a TWIST}

PIZZA JAM?

~~paintball~~ Jam ball →
shoot jam at each other

Wasp-Repelling Jam

Brussels Sprout Jam! →
apple sauce to balance?
perfect for CHRISTmas
(gift dad this year!)

* Try adding peppermint Oil !! ☑

Brussels Sprouts →
cranberry sauce →
← sugar

Too sour cherries = cHerry
B...
Ja...

CAUTION

y
x

LB of Hackney   05/21
9130000143731

First published 2021 by Walker Books Ltd
87 Vauxhall Walk, London SE11 5HJ

2 4 6 8 10 9 7 5 3 1

Text © 2021 Chrissie Sains
Illustrations © 2021 Jenny Taylor

The right of Chrissie Sains and Jenny Taylor to be identified as author and illustrator of this work has been asserted by them in accordance with the Copyright, Designs and Patents Act 1988

This book has been typeset in Stempel Schneidler

Printed and bound by CPI Group (UK) Ltd, Croydon CR0 4YY

British Library Cataloguing in Publication Data: a catalogue record for this book is available from the British Library

ISBN 978-1-4063-9612-6

www.walker.co.uk

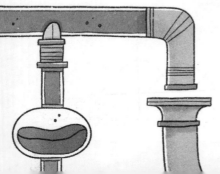

WALKER
BOOKS

FSC
www.fsc.org
MIX
Paper from responsible sources
FSC® C020471

CHAPTER ONE

When Scooter McLay decided to do something, there was very little that anyone could do to stop him. Everything about Scooter screamed determination. From the tips of his unruly red hair, that stuck out as if he'd been plugged into a power socket, to the very ends of his toenails, that grew so quickly he needed to cut them every two days.

Even Scooter's life had started in a rather determined manner.

You see, he hadn't died.

When Scooter's tiny body was first thrust into the world, it was eight long minutes before he took his first breath. Eight minutes of panicked resuscitation, while his parents looked sadly on, quietly fearing that their son's

short life had
already ended.
And then,
just as all hope seemed
lost, Scooter opened his tiny
mouth and took a lungful of air so huge that
his red hair bolted up from his head like
a resplendent bristling bog brush.

It never lay flat from that day forward.

Not when a kindly doctor explained to
Scooter's parents that spending eight minutes
between life and death had led to a condition
called cerebral palsy. And not when that
same doctor went on to say that
even though cerebral palsy was
different for everyone,
it was possible Scooter
might never walk.

But Scooter *could* walk.

True, it had taken years

of special doctors' appointments. His muscles on his left side were a little stiff and he had to wear an uncomfortable splint to stop his left foot from dragging.

But that didn't worry Scooter.

He'd looked death in the face and he'd been the victor. Special doctors' appointments and a splint weren't going to stop him.

What the doctor didn't tell Scooter's parents (because he didn't know this bit) was that those eight minutes had also produced something else:

hyper-creativity.

This meant that Scooter's brain was *full* of ideas. They popped into his head like bubbles in a very fizzy bottle of lemonade.

7

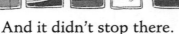

And it didn't stop there.

Those idea bubbles twisted and grew until they were so much more than just an idea. They were whole inventions and calculations and if you popped the top off the lemonade bottle of Scooter's brain, they would fizz out and overflow everywhere.

This proved very useful, given where Scooter grew up.

When Scooter's parents first bought the jam factory (after quitting their jobs at Dodgy Doughnuts next door, where they had to make jam for over a thousand doughnuts from just two strawberries), the plan had simply been to make and sell the most delicious strawberry jam, using as many strawberries as they pleased. There was a flat where they could live just above the factory and a small jam production unit.

But Scooter and his hyper-creativity had changed that.

McLay's Jam now sold over a thousand different flavours of jam.

Not just strawberry, or raspberry, or blackberry.

Oh no.

McLay's Jam sold flavours like Cherry Candy Floss, which melted in your mouth like air. Or Blueberry Burst, which actually felt like a small grenade filled with blueberries had been chucked in your mouth and detonated.

Brussels Sprout Jam had been less successful.

It was supposed to be served with Christmas dinner, but Scooter hadn't quite taken into account just how much everyone hates Brussels sprouts and there had been *a lot* left over.

But Scooter had found a way to use them.

He created a giant Brussels sprout battery, harnessing the power of sprouts and converting it to electricity; enough to power the whole factory.

That was when Scooter began to really experiment.

He started with the Jam Slice. A bit like a cheese slice, but with jam, speeding up the jam sandwich making process by 68.2%.

Next, Jam Smoothie Capsules. Just add milk and create the most delicious jam smoothie.

It was during the testing phase of the capsules that Scooter came up with Jam Ball. A bit like paintball, but with jam.

The only problem with Jam Ball was that you really couldn't play it in wasp season. However, it had led to his latest invention: Wasp-Repelling Jam. Still delicious, but absolutely repellent to wasps, allowing you to eat a jam sandwich in the height of summer with wasps flying right past you.

McLay's Jam was now considered to be the best producer of jam and jam-based inventions in the world.

This was incredibly annoying for Daffy

Dodgy, owner of Dodgy Doughnuts. Her wicked little eyes watched from her office at the top of a tall tower, wishing that she knew the secrets behind their success.

But Scooter thought nothing of Daffy Dodgy. In fact, Scooter had an entirely different problem on his mind right now. A problem that his brain full of ideas hadn't found a solution to just yet. You see, Scooter desperately wanted a pet. But his parents had said no and they didn't appear to be changing their minds.

Not even a little bit.

Every time Scooter suggested a different type of pet, their answer was always the same.

No, Scooter, we're totally obsessed with factory hygiene and actually we're also really mean, so you can't have any kind of pet whatsoever for the rest of your life ever!

OK, so those weren't their exact words. But it was definitely something like that.

That was why Scooter was now standing outside the steel door entrance to the jam inventions laboratory, holding a small snail in the palm of his hand.

In Scooter's typically determined way, he'd decided to prove to his parents that actually he could look after a pet perfectly well. He'd found Gary in a bush three weeks ago and had been looking after him in secret ever since.

Gary wasn't exactly the *perfect* pet. He had a bad habit of sliming onto Scooter's face when he was asleep. It was a bit gross. And he kept trying to escape out of the window. In fact, the only way that

Scooter could keep him in one place was to put a strawberry jam sandwich on a plate at the end of his bed.

Gary loved strawberry jam sandwiches.

Scooter would definitely prefer a dog or a cat, or even a shrimp. But once his parents knew that he'd actually been looking after a pet for three whole weeks without them even realising, how could they refuse?

This time they *had* to agree.

CHAPTER TWO

Daffy Dodgy sat behind her desk, peering down at McLay's Jam from her tower window. She could often be found doing this. One hand holding a telescope to her beady eye, the other stroking a fat white guinea pig that sat dozily on her lap.

"How do they come up with all those ideas, Boris?" she wheezed. "What's their secret? What's inside that factory?"

McLay's Jam looked like an ordinary square building from the outside, but Daffy knew that inside, it was something very special indeed. Not that anyone other than the McLays had ever actually been inside. Well, no further than the entrance hall at least. And that was only very occasional visitors, or perhaps the odd delivery driver.

Daffy hadn't even gotten as far as the entrance hall.

She'd tried to break in, of course. She'd plotted and schemed for years to get inside. But those dastardly McLays had foiled every attempt, increasing their security with each of her failures.

Daffy glanced at the whiteboard, where some of her more recent break-in plans were listed.

JAM-STEALING MASTER PLANS
1. ~~Pretend to be a window cleaner~~: FOILED
   Window alarmed
2. ~~Sneak into a delivery van~~: FOILED
   Scanner on all vans
3. ~~Attach a spy camera to Boris and post him through the letterbox~~: FOILED
   Boris too fat
4. Brick through window?

She sighed. It was a bit embarrassing really.

All the same, they hadn't managed to stop her from gleaning a few titbits of information. If Daffy ever saw anyone entering the factory building, she'd toss down her telescope, buckle up her boots and hotfoot it down there so that when they came out, she could interview them for every little morsel of information about what they had seen.

Apparently, there was an enormous jam fountain in the reception hall, surrounded by jam tarts and marshmallows on sticks. It had three tiers that reached all the way up to the ceiling, each tier trickling a different flavour of jam. From the reception, there was a staircase leading up to the flat where the McLays lived, but it was the two top-secret entrances, each accessed only by fingerprint recognition, that really interested Daffy. One set of doors led to the factory itself, where the jam was made. According to the postie, there was a roller-coaster cart right outside that one. He said that the tracks looped all around the factory and that the cart could stop anywhere. Even

upside down!
But that wasn't
all. A pizza
delivery girl had
told Daffy that she'd glimpsed
inside. She talked of gigantic
robotic hands and tools that
seemed to have a mind of
their own.

Daffy would love to see
inside that factory. She'd love
a ride on that roller coaster if
truth be told. At age 78, Daffy
had never been on a roller
coaster. She'd never even
been on holiday.

She turned her telescope
towards a small blacked-out
window at the back of the
building. Behind that window

was the *most* top-secret room in the whole factory. In fact, it was the very same room that the other entrance led to...

No one had *ever* seen inside that room.

"One day, they'll open that window, Boris." She put down the telescope, let a sleepy Boris slide to the floor and stood up. "Then I'll know their secrets."

Boris squeaked in irritation. He lumbered towards Daffy's slippers under the desk and deposited a little poo pellet in the left slipper.

"They never used to have any ideas when they worked here." Daffy shook her head, thinking back to Mr and Mrs McLay. All she could remember were two fairly mousy, utterly boring individuals. She shrugged, walked to the mirror and patted her perfectly coiffed white hair, her mean eyes twinkling merrily as she brushed down her brown velour tracksuit. Daffy had seven brown velour tracksuits. One for every day of the week, each one of them proudly displaying the word *Dodgy* across her bottom. With a quick sniff of her armpits, she gave herself a little wink in the mirror.

But wait, what was that she saw in the reflection behind her? Quick as lightning she grabbed the telescope.

"It's *open*, Boris!" she cried as the window of the jam inventions lab was thrust open and something thrown out of it. She focused the telescope, then looked at Boris, confused. "I think they just chucked … a *snail* out of the window."

"But, Mum! He's not just a garden snail! He's my *pet* snail! He's *Gary*!"

"Scooter, you *cannot* have a pet snail!" Mum frantically wiped her tongue.

Scooter sighed. This had gone very wrong indeed. One second, he'd been holding Gary in his hand, his little speech about owning a pet all prepared. The next, Gary had launched himself onto Mum's jam sandwich as she lifted it towards her mouth.

Scooter could only watch in horror as Gary, mixed with a half-eaten jam sandwich, had been promptly spat out and lobbed through the window (don't worry, Gary was OK).

22

"I've been looking after him for three weeks, Mum. You hadn't even noticed."

"Why do you want a pet so much anyway?" Mum gave her tongue one last wipe. "Is that *really* what this is about?"

"I dunno." Scooter shrugged. Even though he did really. He plonked himself on a stool and pretended to study the shelves that filled the walls. Anything to avoid Mum's gaze.

The shelves were lined with hundreds upon hundreds of glass jars of jam, all in alphabetical order. Right at the end, two shelves from the top, was a large book.

Every invention he'd ever made or thought of was in that book. He watched as Mum took it down from the shelf and passed it to him with her 'making-up' smile.

"I'm sorry, Scoot." Mum sat quietly beside him. "But when we worked at Dodgy Doughnuts, Daffy's guinea pig used to roam the factory. We had to fish its droppings out of the jam! It was disgusting." She shook her head. "Your dad and I swore that we'd never have *any* animals in our factory." Mum put her hand on his shoulder. "I know it must be hard sometimes, with our rules about security and hygiene. It can't be easy to keep all of this a secret." She looked out of the window, towards the tower looming beside them, the words *Dodgy Doughnuts* blinking above it. "If only that awful Daffy would stop trying to break in. We've put so many security measures in now, she's got to give up soon." She turned back to

Scooter. "You do understand, don't you, Scoot? And ... you're happy, aren't you? You've got plenty of friends at school?"

"Yeah. Course." Scooter nodded. "It's just..."

He looked down at the jam inventions book in his hands.

He'd never shown it to *anyone*.

Well, no one other than his parents, anyway, and they didn't count. The point was, he'd never shown it to any of his friends. He'd never shown any of his friends the factory either. In fact, none of them even knew that he was a jam inventor. Sure, they knew he lived in McLay's Jam factory, the most stupendous jam factory in the world. But they didn't know that it was Scooter who was responsible for all of it.

Scooter understood why it was kept so secure and private. He knew all about their next-door neighbour, Daffy Dodgy and how she would do almost anything to steal his jam recipes.

All the same, it got a little bit lonely sometimes.

That was why he wanted a pet. He could tell a pet all about his

inventions ... all about his ideas ... all about ...
anything really. He wouldn't have to keep
any secrets.

But Mum wouldn't understand.

"Never mind." He stood up, still holding
the jam inventions book, and walked over to
the window. Gary was in a bush eating a leaf.

Scooter sighed. Gary had
never even wanted to be
a pet really. "Are there
really no animals, Mum?
You know, that would
make a good pet?"

Mum thought about it
before shaking her head.

"We've barely got any room left, Scoot.
Your dad and I were just talking last night
about looking for somewhere bigger. Any
pet would have to be tiny ... and clean and
hygienic ... and totally trustworthy in the

factory. I don't think there's an animal on Earth that can be all of those things."

Scooter shut the window.

"I'm gonna have a ride on the roller coaster." He smiled sadly, put the book down and walked towards the door.

Daffy Dodgy sat back and grinned. The jam inventions lab was everything she'd hoped and more, with those brass vats of bubbling jam and shiny pipes all across the ceiling and all those shelves of delicious-looking jam. But what excited her most of all was what she'd seen as Scooter shut the window. He'd been holding a book with two words on the front.

Jam Inventions.

"I need that book, Boris." She squeezed a doughnut in the palm of her hand and watched as the jam trickled down her arm. "And this

time, there's no more Mrs Nicey-Nicey." She eyed a brick lying on the floor. "I'm going to get that recipe book. *Tonight*."

As Daffy schemed and Scooter span and Gary slimed, *something else* was happening far, far away. Something none of them could guess that was about to change *everything*.

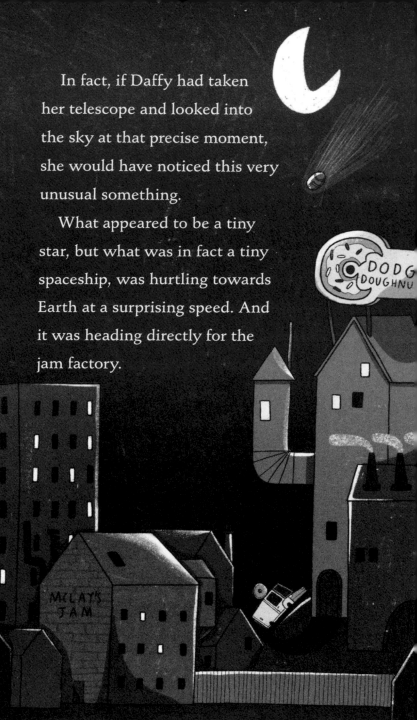

In fact, if Daffy had taken her telescope and looked into the sky at that precise moment, she would have noticed this very unusual something.

What appeared to be a tiny star, but what was in fact a tiny spaceship, was hurtling towards Earth at a surprising speed. And it was heading directly for the jam factory.

CHAPTER THREE

CRASH!

Scooter sat up in bed. What was that? He looked at the clock.

1.42am

There definitely shouldn't be anyone up now. He got out of bed, struggled into his splint and dressing gown and peeked in his parents' room. They were both asleep and snoring.

BANG. Rattle.

The noise was coming from downstairs. *From the factory floor...*

Daffy Dodgy looked at the brick in her hand, then at the unbroken window of the jam inventions lab. It had practically bounced off the glass. She rolled her eyes. Bulletproof glass? Seriously?

But *something* had broken.

"Well, it wasn't us." Daffy pursed her wrinkled lips. "Someone *else* must have broken in."

Boris poked his head out from the tool bag at Daffy's feet. "How did they manage *that*? We'd better find out what's happening, Boris." She kept hold of the brick and began sneaking towards the front of the factory.

Scooter opened the red front door of the tiny flat where he lived with his parents and peered downstairs to the factory reception. Nothing *seemed* out of place. The two doorways leading into the factory and the inventions lab were both securely closed. Everything stood silent and dark. The only light came from the jam fountain as it cheerfully trickled jam into the pool at its base.

He jumped as a cold gust of wind blew onto his cheek.

Was there a window open?

He couldn't tell from up here. He'd better check. Scooter walked carefully down the stairs, and gasped.

The window had a perfect round *hole* in it, about the size of an apple.

He reached out his hand and touched it.

"Ouch!" He pulled his hand away. It was hot!

He peered forwards. It must have been something pretty powerful to get through the bulletproof glass. And it must have been going amazingly fast not to smash the window. That would

have been why the alarm hadn't gone off. But
... *what was it?*

BANG. Rattle.

Scooter turned towards the jam fountain
behind him. Was something over there?
Something definitely moved. Was it a mouse?
He looked back at the hole in the window. A
mutant mouse? A *flying* mutant mouse? He tried
to ignore the shiver down the back of his neck
as he took a silent step forwards, watching
as the something shuffled about near the
jam fountain.

It was ... bright *orange*.

It looked ... well,
actually it looked like
a little orange rubber
ball, but with two
little arms and two
little legs. It had two

antennae and two big round eyes that took up half its face.

It didn't notice Scooter. It was too busy using a marshmallow on a stick to try and scoop out a small metal ball floating at the top of the jam pool.

At least, that's what Scooter thought it was doing.

It was just poking it, really.

"Can I ... help?" Scooter stepped forwards.

The something froze.

Then, quick as a flash, it jumped into a jam tart from the side of the fountain. Its antennae stretched out like a rubber band until they were touching either side of the pastry case. A pulse of light ran through them and to Scooter's total amazement, the little being flew the jam tart into the air like a tiny flying saucer.

"Wait!" Scooter called as it hid inside a vent

above the steel doors into the
jam factory. "I just wanted to help!"
He turned back to the jam fountain, walked
slowly towards it and picked up the small,
jam-covered metal ball.

It was about the size of an apple.

This must be what had made
the hole in the window.

What was it?

A *spaceship?* But it was tiny.
And that would mean ... he
looked up at the vent ... that
would mean that there was ...
an alien in the jam factory.

Scooter put the little
spaceship down, wiped the
jam onto his pyjama leg and
eased himself to the floor.

Why was it here? Had it crash landed? Was it alone? Was it *planning to take over the world*? Scooter didn't think so. In fact, he didn't think that it was really very dangerous at all, seeing as it was hiding right now. Maybe it needed help.

As Scooter pondered this, he didn't notice the jam tart emerge from inside the vent and hover cautiously towards him. In fact, he only noticed when it was just an arm's length away from his face.

The alien and Scooter held each other's gaze for a moment before, slowly, the alien reached down and lifted up some kind of...

Scooter peered forwards.

What *was* that?

It looked a *bit* like a megaphone. Like a tiny version of the one that his PE teacher, Mr Longconk, spoke into on sports day to make it look like he was a professional commentator, when actually it just gave him a way to shout at people even louder than usual.

Scooter watched as the alien lifted it up and aimed it at his face.

Maybe it *wasn't* a megaphone.

Perhaps it was some kind of ray gun and Scooter was about to get blasted into a million tiny pieces. But before he had a chance to consider this further, the alien leant forwards.

"PUT THAT COOKIE DOWN!"

A robotic girl's voice blasted out of it.

Um...

Scooter frowned.

Cookie?

What cookie?

He checked his hands. Nope. No cookies there. He looked behind him. First over one shoulder. Then the other. No.

There were no cookies.

He turned back to the alien, more than a little confused.

She, on the other hand, seemed highly pleased with herself. Raising one eyebrow, she nodded sagely and gave the megaphone a proud little pat. Then she crossed her arms and waited politely for Scooter to reply.

Scooter opened his mouth to say something. Then clamped it shut again.

He peered at the megaphone thing in the alien's hand. Not a ray gun, then. Some kind of shouty tool after all. Perhaps even some kind of alien translator. Except ... well ... except it seemed to be broken. Because, Scooter didn't want to think badly of the alien but, if truth be told, **PUT THAT COOKIE DOWN**, didn't feel like the friendliest of greetings.

The little alien's confident smile dropped, just a little. She glanced sideways at the megaphone and gave it a frustrated little shake.

"Ahoy there!"

Beep.

"Namaste."

WHIRR.

"Howdy Doody."

Crackle.

"WASH YOUR HANDS RIGHT NOW, YOUNG MAN!"

The alien jumped.

Crunch. Beep. Bop.

She shoved it behind her back and fixed a reassuring smile on her face.

"'Sup, homeslice."

The robotic voice came from behind her back.

Scooter giggled.

The alien giggled too, albeit a little sheepishly.

"'Sup." Scooter replied, tilting his head forward and smiling reassuringly. "I'm Scooter." He put his hand to his chest. "*Scoo-ter,*" he repeated.

The alien put the megaphone down beside her on the jam tart, pointed to Scooter with her little arm and repeated softly,

"Scoo-ter."

"Yes! That's right." Scooter nodded.

She put her hand to her chest, just like Scooter had done.

"Fizz-bee." She smiled eagerly.

"Fizzbee," Scooter repeated.

As he spoke her name, her whole face beamed with pleasure. She flew the jam tart into the air in delight, before flying around his head chuckling.

THUD.

"*Ouch.*"

Scooter turned to the window in surprise. What was that? Enough to spook Fizzbee at any rate. The jam tart dived back into the vent with lightning speed.

"Is anyone out there?" he called, walking towards the window.

Nothing.

"Probably just a cat." Scooter gave the window a suspicious glance, then shrugged.

"Scooter?" Dad called from upstairs. "Everything OK? It's the middle of the night, son. What are you doing up? That Dodgy woman isn't trying to break in *again* is she?" Scooter looked towards the vent. Nope, this definitely had *nothing* to do with Daffy Dodgy. All the same, there was no way that he could tell his parents about it. Mum had flipped out about a snail. What would the two of them say about an *alien*?

"No one's trying to break in, Dad," he replied as he leant oh-so-casually on the banister. "I thought I heard a noise, but it was nothing."

Daffy Dodgy crouched down below the
window. She'd been so surprised by the flying
jam tart that she'd dropped the brick on
her foot. She poked her head up and peered
through the window, but that annoying boy
was still there. She quickly ducked back down.

"I can't believe it, Boris," she whispered.
"They've invented *flying jam*!" She stared up
at the small round hole in the window, then
squinted towards the vent. "It flew in there."
She paused, peering towards it. "I wonder if…"
She stopped and grinned. "Boris!" She started
hopping on one foot. "There's something
happening in my head!" She tapped her head
with her thin finger. "Something weird…"
She shook her head. "Boris! I think I've
had … I think it's an *idea*!" She tucked
the tool bag under her arm. "We need to
see inside that factory and find out

where that vent leads." She looked up to the skylight window on the roof of the factory. "Ha!" She grinned. "That ignorant boy just told his dad that we're not here!" She spied an old discarded ladder. "Come on, Boris, they're not going to stop us this time."

CHAPTER FOUR

PINEAPPLES
(80)

"I'm really sorry." Scooter spoke up to the vent. "But I'm not sure that you can stay here. I don't think that my parents…" He pushed over a box, carefully climbed onto it and peered down the vent. "Er… Hello?" There was no sign of her. "Fizzbee?"

Where had she gone?

He'd never really thought about it before, but
there were vent shafts all around the building.
If you were small enough, you could probably
fly straight down them and into…

Uh-oh. He stood back. *The factory*!

He carefully eased Fizzbee's spaceship into
his dressing gown pocket and got into the
roller-coaster cart. He paused, turning back
towards the flat. Should he tell Mum and Dad
about this? No. He could sort it out himself. He
turned back to the roller-coaster control panel.

He pressed *Start* and watched as the steel
doors into the jam factory swung open.

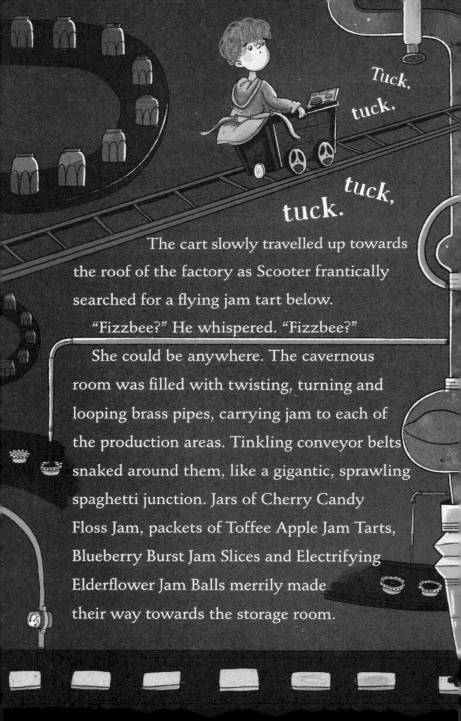

Tuck,

tuck,

tuck,

tuck.

The cart slowly travelled up towards the roof of the factory as Scooter frantically searched for a flying jam tart below.

"Fizzbee?" He whispered. "Fizzbee?"

She could be anywhere. The cavernous room was filled with twisting, turning and looping brass pipes, carrying jam to each of the production areas. Tinkling conveyor belts snaked around them, like a gigantic, sprawling spaghetti junction. Jars of Cherry Candy Floss Jam, packets of Toffee Apple Jam Tarts, Blueberry Burst Jam Slices and Electrifying Elderflower Jam Balls merrily made their way towards the storage room.

All the while, huge robotic hands and tools were washing and measuring, then labelling and packing. It wasn't until Scooter reached the very top of the roller coaster that he saw Fizzbee. She was hovering by the skylight and staring down, her mouth hanging open as if this was the most wonderful thing that she'd ever seen. Scooter couldn't help smiling. It did look pretty amazing from up here. He pressed the stop button.

"That's where we make jam slices." He followed Fizzbee's gaze down to a giant paintbrush, easily the size of a table, directly below them. "The jam goes into that big vat there."

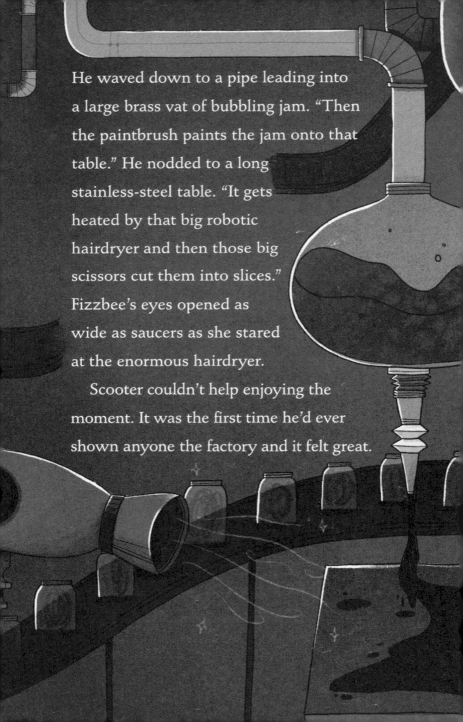

He waved down to a pipe leading into a large brass vat of bubbling jam. "Then the paintbrush paints the jam onto that table." He nodded to a long stainless-steel table. "It gets heated by that big robotic hairdryer and then those big scissors cut them into slices." Fizzbee's eyes opened as wide as saucers as she stared at the enormous hairdryer.

Scooter couldn't help enjoying the moment. It was the first time he'd ever shown anyone the factory and it felt great.

Fizzbee squinted down towards a glass room where you could hear a gentle buzzing sound.

"That's the wasps." Scooter explained. "We make wasp-repelling jam, you see." He waved down to a little conveyor belt carrying open jars of jam past the wasp nests. "It's a really precise calculation so we have to test every jar." He watched as the jam trundled along undisturbed. "We use chilli and peppermint oil because wasps hate both." He nodded at two glasshouses filled with lush green leaves and smiled as Fizzbee's face lit up with wonder.

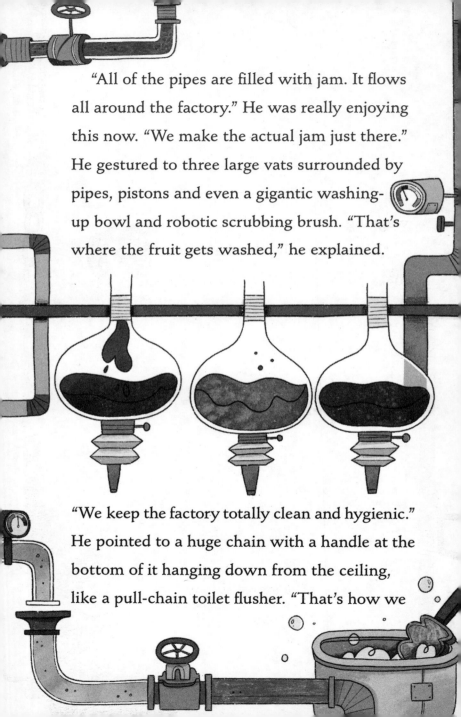

"All of the pipes are filled with jam. It flows all around the factory." He was really enjoying this now. "We make the actual jam just there." He gestured to three large vats surrounded by pipes, pistons and even a gigantic washing-up bowl and robotic scrubbing brush. "That's where the fruit gets washed," he explained.

"We keep the factory totally clean and hygienic." He pointed to a huge chain with a handle at the bottom of it hanging down from the ceiling, like a pull-chain toilet flusher. "That's how we clean everything. We pull on that and all of the equipment gets flushed. I actually designed it all myself," Scooter couldn't help adding.

Fizzbee landed the jam tart in the roller-coaster cart beside Scooter, her antennae wagging.

"It's not actually that hard to make jam." Scooter lay his hand down and smiled as she toddled past his fingers onto his palm. She felt warm and smooth. "It's just fruit and sugar and a few other ingredients all boiled together." He slowly brought his palm in front of his face. "We do have to be quite precise about cooking times because the longer we heat it, the more solid it becomes." He grinned impishly. "Plus, I add a few other ingredients to make the flavours more interesting."

"Jam." Fizzbee spoke slowly, trying to master the new sound.

Scooter looked at her closely. She was *tiny*, no bigger than a Brussels sprout. He thought back to his chat with Mum that morning. She'd said that there were no pets on *Earth* that could live in the factory.

Well, Fizzbee wasn't from Earth.

In fact, Fizzbee wasn't even a pet. Fizzbee was an alien. That was a *million times* cooler than having a pet. She was a friend *from a whole other planet*. And it wasn't even like Scooter could get the blame for bringing her into the factory. She brought herself here! Plus, where would she go if she didn't stay? What if she got into trouble, or if something happened to her? Scooter couldn't live with himself if that happened.

All the same, he had a sneaking suspicion that

Mum and Dad *might* see things a *bit* differently.

His eyes met Fizzbee's.

It *would* be nice if she could stay. He could show her more of the factory and his inventions. Maybe Mum and Dad wouldn't mind so much if she knew the factory rules, if he'd trained her up a bit? He'd probably be saving them a lot of worry. They might even thank him for handling the situation so well.

"Do you want to stay here?" He whispered.

Fizzbee looked at him blankly.

"You." Scooter held his hand out towards her. Fizzbee looked down at Scooter's open hand, then frowned and shook her head. She put her hand to her chest.

"Fizz-bee." She spoke slowly, as though speaking to a small child.

"Oh! Er. Right. No. That's not what I meant." Scooter shook his head. "Let's start again." He held his hand towards her again.

"Fizzbee." She nodded.

"Stay." He paused. How could he act out *staying*? He started by pretending to be asleep, then acted waking up, stretching and eating food.

Fizzbee blinked.

"Er... Here?" He spread his arms wide to indicate the factory.

Fizzbee looked around the factory, then back at Scooter.

"Fizzbee ... stay ... here?" He repeated with the actions.

Fizzbee gave him a puzzled smile before looking down at the megaphone translator in her  hand. She lifted it up, turned it around and put it over her ear like an old-fashioned ear trumpet. Then she gave Scooter a thumbs up.

Scooter looked at her dubiously. Wasn't that thing broken? What if it started shouting about cookies again? But Fizzbee seemed to think it would work. She bobbed her head encouragingly towards him.

Scooter leant forward and spoke slowly and loudly. "Do you want to stay here?"

The megaphone ear trumpet made a low humming noise. Had it worked? Fizzbee concentrated for a moment, then her face lit up and she nodded eagerly.

"Is that what your language sounds like?" Scooter tried to repeat the humming noise, then stopped as Fizzbee's eyes opened wide. Like he'd said a rude word or something.

"Oh." He blushed. "Sorry. Anyway... I think it's probably best if we keep this a secret for now, until you're settled in at least. We'll tell my mum and dad in a few days." He added, "OK?"

Fizzbee shrugged and nodded.

"Cool." Scooter grinned broadly as Fizzbee tossed the megaphone ear trumpet over her shoulder, jumped back into the jam tart, zipped up into the air, circled his head and flew down towards the factory floor.

He leant forwards and pressed the start button on the roller coaster.

Daffy hobbled unsteadily up
the ladder and peered into the
skylight window.

"Boris!" She gasped at the
sight of the factory below.
"It's amazing." She stared at
the pipes, conveyor belts and
huge robotic tools, and felt sick
with jealousy. Her factory was
nothing like this. Her factory
was dull and dirty and *ordinary*.

61

What she saw below her was magical.

The little jam tart zipped past the skylight, before flying down towards the factory floor. "It must have got in through that vent. I *knew* there'd be a way in." She stared longingly through the window. "If only *I* was small enough to get in through those vents, Boris." She glanced down at him as he nibbled uninterestedly on a stale doughnut he'd found in her tool bag. "Hang on..." her eyes flared with a new idea. "*You* are!"

Boris eyed her warily.

"No more doughnuts." She pulled the doughnut away and threw it to the ground. "From now on, you're on a strict diet. And we'd better start training you up." She studied the factory below one last time, making a mental note of the alarm wires and Brussels battery, before climbing back down the ladder.

"We're not just going to steal their recipe book, Boris. We're going to put them out of business altogether!"

CHAPTER
FIVE

"So, there are a few rules." Scooter pressed the stop button, bringing the cart to a halt by the doors. "Rule one: you can't touch any of the jam in the actual factory."

He looked for the little megaphone ear trumpet. They'd probably need that if he was going to explain the rules properly. It was nowhere to be seen. Come to think of it, Fizzbee seemed to have disappeared too.

"Fizzbee?"

"Wheeeeeeeeeeeeeeee!" Fizzbee dived from a pipe, cannon-balling into a bubbling vat of Blueberry Burst Jam.

SPLASH.

She swam around the vat, blowing bubbles and covering herself in jam as if it were a soapy bubble bath.

"You can't swim in there!" Scooter hurried towards her. Fizzbee stopped swimming and splashed some jam towards him playfully.

He sighed, this would be much easier with

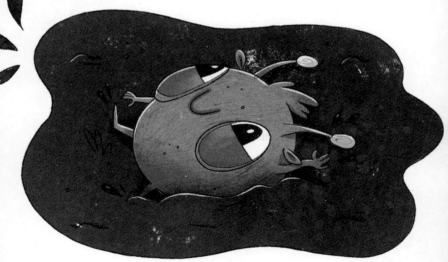

the translator thing. "Look, if you want to stay here, you're going to have to—"

GURGLE, GRUMBLE, **GROWL**.

Fizzbee stopped swimming. Her eyes darted down towards her stomach.

"What was that?" Scooter asked warily as Fizzbee wriggled her belly.

GURGLE, GRUMBLE, **GROWL**.

It was louder this time.

"Are you … hungry?" He rubbed his tummy to show her what he meant.

Fizzbee nodded.

"OK. So, what do you normally eat? You know, where you come from?"

Fizzbee answered simply by taking out a straw from … well, Scooter had no idea where the straw came from, but there was definitely a straw.

"I don't think that's a good—" he watched

as Fizzbee dipped the straw into the jam. "And anyway, you can't eat the—"

She began sucking up the Blueberry Burst Jam like an industrial vacuum cleaner.

Scooter's mouth fell open as the vat of jam began to slowly disappear, while Fizzbee continued slurping and swiggling and swalogging, yet remaining *exactly the same size*.

"How are you doing that?" he asked in amazement. "Where's the jam *going*?"

Fizzbee continued sucking at the straw until the vat was entirely empty. She smiled from the bottom of the vat and let out a small burp.

"I know I said that you can stay." Scooter handed a jam tart down to her and watched as she flew up towards him. "But my parents are another matter. And I can tell you now, they'll never agree if you start swimming in the jam vats and then eating it all up with a straw. If you want to stay, then we're going to have to—" He stopped.

Fizzbee was changing colour. She was turning … *purple*.

"Does that normally happen after you eat?" Scooter frowned.

Fizzbee looked down at her tummy and wriggled. She gulped, then wriggled again.

SPLAT.

The jam tart fell to the floor.

Though Fizzbee was still
hovering in the air, her little arms
and legs flapping about, her eyes
wide and frightened.

"Are you OK?"

She pulled her arms and legs in and closed
her eyes tight, as though she knew something
was about to happen and it was going to be
something bad.

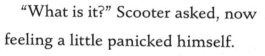

"What is it?" Scooter asked, now
feeling a little panicked himself.

He didn't have to wait long for
the answer.

Fizzbee began to ping around
the factory like a little purple ball in a
giant game of pinball.

Donk.

Scooter flinched as she
bounced off a pipe above.

BANG.

69

She knocked into
the jam ball moulds.

Whoosh.

Scooter ducked as she
sped past his ear.

CLANG.

She landed in a huge
mixing bowl in the jam tart production area.

"Scooooo-terrrrrrrrr!" she shouted as she
ran around the mixing bowl, orange again
now, desperately trying to escape a giant
wooden spoon as it tried to stir her into a
pastry mix. The bowl automatically tilted and
shook her out onto a table where a gigantic
rolling pin lurched towards her.

"Scooooo-terrrrrrrrr!" she cried again as
she ran down the table, her hands waving
in the air.

Scooter pressed the **EMERGENCY STOP**
button and watched as the machinery slowly
came to a halt.

"Scooter?"

Dad stood at the factory doors, his brown
hair sticking up, one pyjama
leg gathered around his knee.
He sighed and rubbed his eyes.
"What's going on, Scoot? I
know it's the weekend
tomorrow, but you still
need your sleep."

"Sorry, Dad." Scooter
felt something land in
the hood of his dressing
gown. Then the scramble
of two little arms and
legs climbing into his
unruly hair. "I didn't
realise the time."

Dad scratched the top of his head, before glancing around the factory. "Well, back to bed now then, son." He sighed.

"Night, Dad." Scooter pulled himself up the stairs to the flat one step at a time. His leg was aching a bit beneath the splint. "Stay hidden there for a minute," he whispered to Fizzbee. There was no response. "Umm … are you still up there?" He carefully raised his hand, before hearing a loud, snoring noise.

Zzzzzzz-shew. Zzzzzzzz-shew. Zzzzzzzz-hngGGggh-Ppbhww.

"Oh." Scooter brought his hand back down. "You're asleep. Well, I guess you'd better stay there for now."

But when Scooter got back to his room, instead of going back to bed, he sat thoughtfully at his desk. True, it wasn't going to be easy getting to sleep with a little alien snoozing in his hair, but that wasn't what troubled Scooter.

If he was going to have any chance of convincing Mum and Dad to let Fizzbee stay, then she needed some serious training. He turned to his tablet and stylus on his desk, opened a new note and typed:

OPERATION: TRAIN FIZZBEE

To start with, he'd have to find out what Fizzbee could actually eat. He couldn't have her ping-ponging around the place again. Then he'd need to make sure she understood the factory rules, especially about hygiene and cleanliness. Maybe he could show her how to use the bath or the shower. He paused. *Did she know how to use the toilet?* He pulled open his dressing gown pocket and peered down at her spaceship. Maybe she had a toilet in there? There was a quiet grunt from the top of his head as Fizzbee rolled over in her sleep and Scooter closed his pocket with a protective pat. He took out the factory training manual from his desk drawer and started making notes. Tomorrow would be a busy day.

CHAPTER SIX

Bright and early the next morning, Daffy Dodgy stood in front of Boris like a sergeant major addressing her troops. Her foot was covered in a large bandage. It still hurt.

"Right then, Boris." She pointed to the top of the whiteboard behind her, where she had written the words:

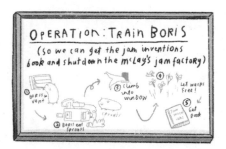

OPERATION: TRAIN BORIS
(so we can get the jam inventions book and shut down the McLay's jam factory)

① Boris in vent
② Boris eat sprouts
③ climb into window
④ let wasps free!
⑤ Get book

Followed by a fairly poorly drawn step-by-step plan of action.

"The plan is simple." Daffy tapped the whiteboard with her pen.

"One: you are going to get into the factory through the vents." She tapped a picture of the Brussels battery. "Two: you are going to eat the Brussels sprouts that power the alarm so that I can sneak in through the window of the jam inventions lab." She tapped the third point of the plan and smirked. "The next bit is my favourite part." She paused dramatically. "Four: you are going to release all of the wasps into the factory." She let out a squeal of delight. "Ha! It's the perfect diversion while I steal the book!" She pointed to number five. "The wasps will probably wreck half the machinery. It'll take weeks to fix everything!" She picked Boris up and began to dance with him across the room. "By the time they re-open, I'll have copied all of their recipes!

1 BORIS in vent

2 BORIS eat sprouts

3 climb into window

4 Let wasps free!

dig tunnel under factory

plunger breaks away

Dodgy Doughnuts will have
the best jam-filled doughnuts in
the world! We'll sell flying doughnuts,
exploding doughnuts, even doughnuts that

make your hair stand on end!"
She twirled. "Nobody will want
McLay's Jam any more. Not when
they can have one of our brand new *Daring
Dodgy Doughnuts*! Ha!" She took a deep breath
to calm herself down.

"But it's going to take some training, Boris."
She placed him back on her desk,
then glanced at her notepad where
she'd jotted some kind of training
schedule. She pointed to the first
item: *sprout speed-eating*. "You're
going to have to eat a shedload of
sprouts to power down the alarm."
She emptied a huge sack of sprouts
onto the floor before taking a

stopwatch out of her pocket. "Let's see how long it takes you to get through these." She clicked the timer.

"Tomorrow—" she pointed to a homemade tunnel of upside-down boxes and the treadmill—"we start on vent navigation and conveyor belt fitness training."

Boris blinked twice and dropped a poo pellet.

"That's it, Boris, make room for those sprouts." Daffy patted him on the head. "Oh, and I don't want you worrying about what's going to happen when you release those wasps into the factory." Boris inched backwards as Daffy lifted a fishing rod, an old teddy dressed as a wasp stuck to the end of it. "This is for wasp avoidance training." She smiled reassuringly.

Meanwhile, Scooter was only just waking up.

He lifted his head groggily from his desk, stretched and yawned. He dressed, which took a bit of concentration, and for a moment he completely forgot... His hand flew to his hair.

Where was Fizzbee?

He looked around his bedroom, wide awake now. All of his books were scattered across the floor. As if someone had *broken in*!

"Fizzbee?" he whispered.

No reply.

"Fizzbee?" he repeated, a little more urgently now. *Where was she?* Had something happened to her? Had she run away? Had she gone into the kitchen? What if Mum and Dad saw her?

A small trail of crumbs led out of his bedroom door. He stood up and followed them towards the *bathroom?*

"Fizzbee?" he whispered into the closed door. "Fizzbee? Are you in there?"

SHWOOOOSHHHHHHHHHHHH GURGLE GURGLE SWISH.

The toilet flushed.

He pressed his ear to the door and listened as someone pressed the soap dispenser, then turned on the tap and washed their hands.

SSSHHHHHHHHSSSSSSHHHHHHHH.

That was the shower!

Was Fizzbee even in there? He had to find out. He lifted his hand to the handle…

"Jammy jammy jammy jaaaaaaaammmmmm. Oh jaaaaaaaam. I love yoooouuuuuuuuuu."

His hand hung in mid-air.

"Oh Scoooooterrrrrr I love you tooooooooooooo."

Was that *Fizzbee*? It sounded a *bit* like Fizzbee. Though she seemed to have learnt some new words. Did that mean that she knew how to use the shower? And the *toilet*?

After a short while, the bathroom door opened and Fizzbee flew out in her jam tart, smelling distinctly of Dad's shower gel. She stopped when she saw Scooter and smiled.

"Good morning, Scooter." She spoke perfectly. "Fizzbee is clean and hygienic." She puffed her chest out, then flew into his bedroom and landed on his desk. She picked up the factory training manual and began … *reading* it.

"Did you—" Scooter surveyed the carnage of books on the floor—"do this?"

"Yes." Fizzbee looked up and nodded, before returning to her reading.

"Did you *read them*?"

"Yes." She nodded again. "Fizzbee has read all of your books. Fizzbee has made notes. Fizzbee very much likes the aliens that wear underpants." She chuckled. "Verrrrry funny." She pointed down to the factory training manual. "Now Fizzbee learns the factory rules."

"Oh." Scooter watched as she flicked through the manual with surprising speed. Much faster than he could read at any rate. "Well, that's *brilliant*!" He grinned, seeing her with new eyes. "I didn't realise that you're so... I mean... I didn't think..." He stopped as Fizzbee raised her eyes towards him, suddenly feeling more than a little ashamed of himself. It hadn't occurred to him that Fizzbee could read.

Or that she could figure out how to use the toilet and the shower.

Or that she might not need him to train her ... because she was smart enough to train herself.

"I'm really sorry." He glanced down at his left leg. "People underestimate me sometimes too." He shook his head, frowning. "I should have known better. I haven't actually asked what *you* want, have I? Or why you're here? Or where you come from? Have I even said welcome to Earth? Because I really should have done..." He trailed off.

Fizzbee padded into her jam tart and flew up to his shoulder.

"It's OK, Scooter." She patted his ear sympathetically. "Fizzbee is sorry too. Fizzbee broke the rules." She glanced over to the factory manual. "Fizzbee promises not to break the rules ever again."

GURGLE, GRUMBLE, **GROWL.**

"Oh no." Scooter looked at her tummy. "You're not hungry *again* are you?"

"A little bit." She smiled nervously.

"Do you have any food, you know, in your spaceship?"

Fizzbee shook her head.

"Well, do you know what you can actually eat? Because I don't think Blueberry Burst Jam was all that good for you."

"Yes." Fizzbee nodded eagerly. "There are two things that Fizzbee can eat on Earth."

"OK." Scooter waited. "So … what are they?"

"Number one food." Fizzbee raised her hand. "Is jam." She beamed.

"Excellent." Scooter brightened. "Well you're in the right place. So ... what type of jam exactly?" Fizzbee shrugged, a slightly pained smile on her face. "Because there are quite a few flavours," Scooter continued. "Like ... *thousands.*"

"Er ... Jam flavour?" Fizzbee giggled awkwardly.

"R-i-i-ght." Scooter rubbed his forehead. "So, what's the other food that you can eat?"

"Number two food." Fizzbee raised her other hand. "Is a size two slipper that has taken exactly 432 and a half steps."

"*Really*?" Scooter pulled a face. "Where did you get this information? Are you *sure*?"

"Yes." Fizzbee nodded, one eyebrow raised. "Fizzbee is totally sure."

"What about if there was a slipper that had taken 433 steps?"

"No, Scooter." She looked at him as if he had asked a particularly stupid question. "Not good. Not good at all."

"I'm a size two. Is my slipper all right?" Scooter

picked up his slipper from the floor and held it towards her. She hovered forwards and gave it a cautious sniff.

"No." She shook her head sharply.

"Oh. Right." Scooter tossed the slipper away. "I guess we should stick with jam then."

"Yes." Fizzbee agreed.

"We'd better get to the lab in that case." Scooter walked towards his bedroom door, but as he reached for the handle, Fizzbee stopped him. Her eyes drifted up to his unruly red hair, then over to the factory training manual.

"Rule Six. You must wear hairnet when preparing food." She raised her eyebrows. "Where is Scooter's hairnet?"

CHAPTER SEVEN

"Come on, Boris!" Daffy looked at the stopwatch in her hand and sighed. It had been exactly one hour, 32 minutes and 14 seconds and Boris had eaten precisely *zero* sprouts.

"They're not that bad, really." Daffy picked one up and sniffed it suspiciously before eyeing Boris again.

He crossed his paws, put his head to one side and gave her his most moody look.

Totally unimpressed.

Daffy took a tiny nibble of the sprout.

"Urgh." She spat it out. "Oh, all right then, they taste like feet." She sighed and sat down heavily on her desk chair. Boris clearly needed some high-level motivation.

"I know you don't like them," she said picking him up. "Nobody likes them much." She put him on her desk and leant down to talk to him, woman to guinea pig. "But you need to eat through the Brussels battery if this plan's going to work and, anyway, you'll get stuck in the vents if you don't lose a few ounces."

Boris squeaked grumpily, before turning away from her.

Daffy opened the desk drawer and took out a small, rectangular jewellery box.

"I *was* saving this for your birthday." She held it up. "But maybe you could have it early … if you help me."

She opened it with a flourish as Boris turned  curiously towards it. Inside was a pink sparkly heart pendant with *Best Friends* written on it in silver lettering. He rolled his eyes.

"**Squeeak.**" He turned his bottom towards her.

"I thought you'd love it!" Daffy took it out of the box. "Look! It splits into two halves. One for me and one for you." She held it out towards him.

Boris picked up the heart pendant in his mouth, lumbered towards the edge of the desk

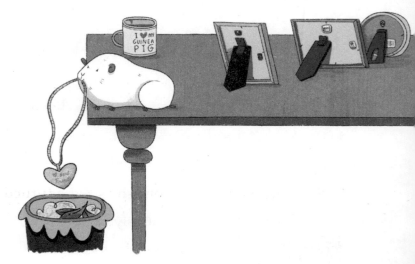

and dropped it in the bin. Daffy looked down at the bin, then back at Boris.

"Does that mean you'll start training?"

"**Squeeak**." Boris edged his bottom over the desk and released a poo pellet into the bin. Daffy was pretty sure that meant 'no'. She sighed and put the jewellery box back in her desk drawer next to a squeezy bottle of *Just for Guinea Pigs Non-Toxic Chocolate Sauce* that she kept for when Boris deserved a special treat. She pulled it out and looked at it thoughtfully.

"**Squeeak**." Boris stood, staring hungrily at

the chocolate sauce bottle, his eyes alert, his bottom wagging.

"You want this?" Daffy waved the chocolate sauce bottle temptingly. Boris panted in anticipation. "Right-o." Daffy picked up one solitary Brussels sprout and placed it carefully on her desk. She let Boris watch as she slowly drizzled chocolate sauce onto it. Boris sniffed it cautiously. He locked eyes with Daffy, nodded, then hoovered up the sauce-covered sprout in seconds.

"Excellent, Boris!" Daffy grinned as she drizzled chocolate sauce onto the rest of the pile of sprouts. "Let's do that again."

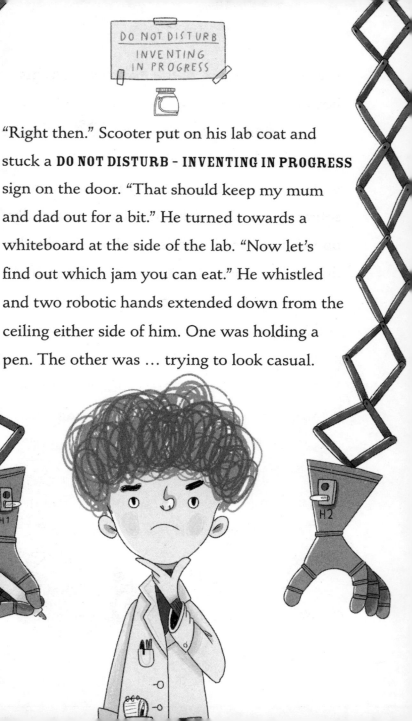

"Right then." Scooter put on his lab coat and stuck a **DO NOT DISTURB - INVENTING IN PROGRESS** sign on the door. "That should keep my mum and dad out for a bit." He turned towards a whiteboard at the side of the lab. "Now let's find out which jam you can eat." He whistled and two robotic hands extended down from the ceiling either side of him. One was holding a pen. The other was … trying to look casual.

Fizzbee stood on Scooter's workbench. She looked from Scooter to the robotic hands, then back to Scooter, a slightly confused smile fixed on her face.

"Oh, sorry." Scooter placed his hand down on the desk and felt a warm tickle on his palm as she climbed onto it. "These are my Hand-Bots." He brought his hand up reassuringly. "I developed them to help me. My hands can be a bit stiff sometimes and my  handwriting is so messy. The Hand-Bots make things easier." The two hands gave Fizzbee a friendly wave. "I've coded them to have a bit of personality," he said, smiling. "And they respond to my voice commands: Hand-Bot Two, can you put this somewhere for us, please?"

Scooter eased Fizzbee's spaceship out of his pocket and handed it to the penless robotic hand. They watched as it placed the spaceship on a shelf next to a jar of Sherbet Lemon Jam.

"There's a jar of every jam flavour that we've ever made on these shelves." Scooter lifted his hand to show her as Hand-Bot One made notes. "If we work our way through them, then we should be able to figure out which ones you can eat. Let's start with Cherry Candy Floss." Hand-Bot Two took down a jar from the shelves and opened it. "It's really light and airy." Scooter continued. "So, I'm hoping it won't have any effect on you." He put his hand back onto his workbench and let Fizzbee jump down, before grabbing a saucepan and sticking it on his head. "Just in case."

He smiled apologetically as Hand-Bot Two carefully lifted a spoonful of jam towards Fizzbee as though it was medicine.

She looked at it for a moment, before poking out her tiny orange tongue and taking the tiniest, weeniest little lick of it. She rolled the jam around inside her mouth, then grinned and licked her lips appreciatively.

"Yes, Scooter. Fizzbee likes Cherry Candy Floss Jam verrry..."

POP.

Scooter blinked.

Fizzbee's little round body had quadrupled in size and puffed up like an inflated balloon.

She giggled nervously as she started to float up towards the ceiling.

"Make a note please, Hand-Bot One." Scooter watched as the robotic hand holding the pen unravelled a long list of jam flavours and put a sharp cross through 'Cherry Candy Floss'.

Scooter turned back to Fizzbee as Hand-Bot Two gently tried to pull her down from the ceiling.

"Don't worry." He glanced down the length of the list. "We've still got loads more to try."

CHAPTER EIGHT

Boris scurried along the treadmill as fast as his little legs could carry him. It was the second morning of the schedule; vent and conveyor belt navigation training.

"Jump off now, Boris." Daffy coached him. "Over to the Blueberry Burst pipe." She pointed to a line of toilet rolls taped together, meant to represent the pipe. "Then you just need to tiptoe across until you reach the Brussels

battery." Daffy pointed to an upside-down box, the words *Brussels Battery* scrawled on the side of it.

Boris glanced sideways at the toilet-roll pipe and pounded on. He didn't much fancy jumping off the cliff edge of the treadmill onto what was virtually a tightrope made of bog rolls.

"Will you do it for a chocolate-covered sprout?" Daffy waved a sprout at the end of the pipe.

"Squeeak."

Boris shook his head grumpily. Chocolate sauce-covered sprouts weren't quite so appealing after he'd eaten a sack full of them yesterday.

OPERATION: TRAIN BORIS
(so we can get the jam inventions book and shutdown the M'Lay's jam factory)

"There's got to be something that will convince you." Daffy scanned the room, until her eyes rested on the sparkly pink *Best Friends* pendant, still in the bin.

"Look, Boris." She fished it out. "I don't think you realise how special this is. It's a representation of our everlasting…"

But Boris wasn't listening. At the sight of the glistening pendant he launched himself off the treadmill and jumped for dear life. Anything to avoid Daffy trying to put that thing on him again.

"Oh, Boris!" Daffy cried with delight. "I knew you loved it really!"

Scooter and Fizzbee flopped down together
onto his desk chair. They'd been up since dawn
testing hundreds of jams and Fizzbee had
floated, foamed, flamed, flipped, fizzled and,
finally, farted (so loudly it had almost rattled
Scooter's eyes out of his head). Even plain old
strawberry jam had brought her out in a flush
of fuchsia spots.

"At least you haven't been hungry." Scooter
shrugged. "But maybe a size two slipper that
has taken precisely 432 and a half steps would
have been easier." His gaze travelled down the
list, a slightly sinking feeling inside of him.

There was just one jam left to try: Brussels Sprout Jam. Scooter had a feeling that this could go very wrong indeed. After all, Brussels sprouts had enough energy inside them to power the whole factory, not to mention the slightly *windy* effect they had on most people. But *Fizzbee*? What would it do to *her*?

"Are you sure you want to try this one?"

"Yes." Fizzbee's mouth set in a firm line. "This is the last jam. This must be the one that Fizzbee can eat."

"I hope so." Scooter watched with no small sense of unease as the Hand-Bots reached up for the jar of sticky green gloop, took out a

spoonful and inched it ever so carefully towards Fizzbee's open mouth. Scooter pulled the saucepan tight over his head, knelt down behind his workbench and squeezed his eyes shut.

Nothing.

He waited a bit longer.

Still nothing.

He opened his eyes and took a cautious peek over the barricade.

"It's OK, Scooter!" Fizzbee stood on the workbench smiling. "Fizzbee feels nothing but..."

GRRRRRRRRRRRRRRRRRRRRRRRRRRRR-BLPA-GLOOOGA.

Was that Fizzbee's tummy rumbling? Uh-oh. Scooter ducked back down.

GLUGALUGLUGALUG-SSSHHHHHHHHH-PAH-PAAAAHHHHHHH.

Silence.

Scooter peeked back up to see Fizzbee patting her tummy.

"Please excuse Fizzbee." She blushed.

"That's a relief." Scooter stood up as the Hand-Bots did a fist bump. "I was starting to wonder if we'd ever find a jam for you. I think I might develop some Brussels Sprout Jam Slices in that case." The Hand-Bots took down the jam inventions book and picked up a pen ready to write a note for him.

"What is this, Scooter?" Fizzbee pointed as Scooter opened the book, revealing pages and pages of his ideas and… "Inventions!" Fizzbee gasped, her eyes wide in wonder.

"Yes, that's right." Scooter took the saucepan off his head. "All of the inventions I've ever made are in this book." He smiled. It felt nice to share his inventions with a friend. Someone who could see all the things he'd made. Someone who could see *all* of him. Not just Scooter with the bog-brush red hair, *or* Scooter who wore a splint, *or* Scooter the jam inventor. But all of those things. Was Fizzbee that friend? He watched as she began flicking through the book.

"That first section is for my successful recipes." Scooter explained.

Successful RECIPES
* Peanut butter and Jelly (half jam, half jelly) Tarts
* Jam Dip
* Jam Fountain
* Edible jam paper (for pass the parcel)

Fizzbee scanned the page then turned to the next section. "That part is for my not so successful inventions." Scooter pulled a face. There were fewer recipes here.

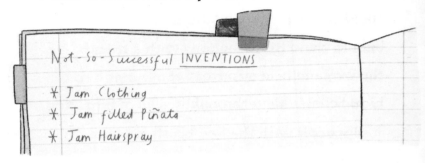

Not-So-Successful INVENTIONS

＊ Jam Clothing
＊ Jam filled Piñata
＊ Jam Hairspray

"That last section—" he said as Fizzbee turned to the final part of the book—"is for my inventions-in-progress."

He tapped the top of the page.

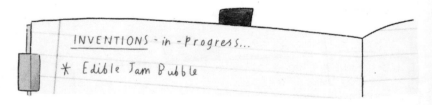

INVENTIONS-in-Progress...

＊ Edible Jam Bubble

"It's my latest idea." Scooter grinned. "Bubble mix made of jam and you can eat the bubbles." He walked over to two small bubbling vats of strawberry jam at the end of his workbench.

"These are my testing vats," he explained as Hand-Bot One lifted a large bubble wand from one of the vats and held it in front of him. Scooter blew through it.

Ppppffffffffffff.

Tiny jam bubbles puffed out, almost immediately popping to nothing.

"The bubbles pop too quickly." Hand-Bot One put the bubble wand back in the vat. "I need to find a way to make them bigger *before* they pop."

Fizzbee looked down at the recipe, then back up at Scooter, her antennae wagging excitedly.

"Scooter!" She jumped up and down, wriggling her bottom gleefully. "Fizzbee can help! Fizzbee knows how to make the jam bubbles bigger."

"Really? You mean, you can help me?"

"Yes, Scooter." She nodded. "This is why Fizzbee is here."

CHAPTER NINE

Daffy watched as Boris completed ten one-pawed press-ups on each side before punching a miniature wasp-shaped punching bag. She lowered the fishing rod towards him and grinned as Boris commando rolled out of the way, squished his head and front paws inside an empty jam jar, then crawled forwards, using the jam jar as a shield from the wasp-dressed teddy.

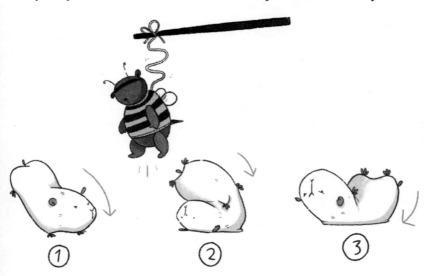

① ② ③

"You're ready, Boris." She helped him out of the jar. "We'll do the job tonight." She put him on her lap and stroked his soft white fur. "You really are my best friend, you know?" She lifted the *Best Friends* pendant, took her half, attached it to a necklace and put it on proudly. "Now your turn."

Attaching the other half to a pink diamante collar, she held it out and smiled lovingly.

Boris looked at the collar and the pendant, then up at Daffy's eager face and smiled back.

Nice try.

He turned, kicked it with his back leg and Daffy watched as it sailed through the air and slam-dunked into the bin.

"Well, I'm still going to wear my half," she grumbled.

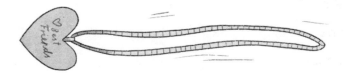

Scooter watched as Fizzbee flew up to her
spaceship, landed the jam tart and pressed
her antennae against the round metal ball.
He gasped as a door opened and a tiny metal
staircase emerged. Fizzbee waved, before
climbing inside, rustling around for a while
and heaving out what could only be described
as a large brown suitcase. Large for Fizzbee
anyway, not so much for Scooter. But all
the same, it appeared to be *bigger* than her
spaceship.

"How did you fit that in there?" Scooter peered up towards her. Fizzbee didn't answer. She simply lifted the suitcase into the jam tart and flew unsteadily back down to Scooter's workbench.

"These are Fizzbee's inventions." She smiled proudly.

"You mean *you're an inventor too*?" Scooter beamed. This just got better and better!

"Yes." Fizzbee nodded. She opened her suitcase as though it were a chest packed with precious treasure. It was bursting with tiny sparkling glass bottles, each of them filled with glittering liquids of every colour. Scooter watched as she pulled out a small blue vial.

"This will make the bubbles bigger." Fizzbee grinned, popped the top off

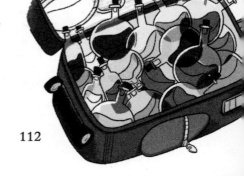

the vial and poured a drop into the edible jam bubble mix.

"Try now." She waited eagerly.

Hand-Bot One lifted the bubble wand once again and Scooter blew.

A perfect rainbow coloured bubble gently blossomed out of the bubble wand, before detaching and floating across the room.

"*No way!*" Scooter watched as it bobbed towards the window and bumped softly against the glass. "It didn't pop!" he exclaimed, as it continued bouncing lightly against the pane. Hand-Bot Two opened the window, releasing it into the blue sky outside, and Scooter smiled as it floated up and down like a balloon. It meandered slowly towards a small snail in the bushes outside … but not just any snail.

"Gary!" Scooter waved to his former pet as the bubble hovered above him.

He stopped mid-wave and frowned as the bubble slowly descended over Gary until the little snail was ... *inside* the bubble.

It began to float up into the air, Gary still inside.

"Er... Is it going to pop?" Scooter watched as the bubble floated gently up, carrying a disgruntled-looking Gary with it.

"Yes." Fizzbee replied with absolute certainty.

"When?"

"One hour ... or three?" She shuffled her feet slightly awkwardly. "Fizzbee is not completely sure."

"Hmmm." Scooter made a mental note to leave a jam sandwich out for Gary later as an apology. "Well, it might need a *bit* more work," he paused. "But we could work on that together, once we've told Mum and Dad about you." He smiled. "I think it's time. I don't see how they could say no. It's not like you take up any room and you know the factory rules better than I do!" He patted the hairnet Fizzbee had helped him put on. "We could work together on inventions. It's perfect!"

"Fizzbee would like that, Scooter." She raised her eyes towards him shyly and went to close her suitcase.

"Wait a minute." Scooter stopped her. "We can go and tell them in a bit. Why don't you show me some more of your inventions first?"

"Oh yes!" Fizzbee's antennae wagged excitedly. "Fizzbee will show you."

As she turned back to the suitcase and began busily rummaging around inside, neither Scooter, nor Fizzbee noticed as her excited antennae brushed past the blue vial of liquid. For a moment, it swayed on the edge of the workbench, then tipped over and slowly emptied its contents into a plant pot.

"Ah-ha!" Fizzbee pulled out another tiny bottle from her suitcase, this time filled with a bright purple liquid. She poured a drop into the second testing vat of strawberry jam, stirred it with a wooden spoon, then lifted out a spoonful and handed it to Scooter.

"Scooter try it." She nodded eagerly, never taking her eyes off his face.

Scooter took the spoon and lifted it towards his mouth.

He paused.

"Are you sure this is a good idea?"

"Yes! Yes!" Fizzbee was practically jumping up and down she was so excited. Scooter peered at the spoonful of jam in his hand, then back at Fizzbee.

"Have you tried this on a human before?"

"Er. No." She shook her head.

"Then maybe I shouldn't…" He stopped as Fizzbee's antennae drooped. "Oh, never mind." He shoved the spoonful of jam in his mouth.

It tasted exactly the same as usual.

Delicious, of course (Scooter prided himself on his standard strawberry jam recipe) but still just the same.

"Was something supposed to happen?" He looked at Fizzbee. "Because…"

He paused. Was it his imagination or was the hairnet getting bigger on his head? In fact, everything seemed to be a little bit bigger.

"Fizzbee?" He pulled the hairnet off and dropped it on the floor. "What's ha…?" There was a tingling sensation and a sucking noise, like a slow puncture in a tyre and suddenly he was…

Where was he?

The walls were filled with shelves of colourful jam jars, except they were huge! Almost as big as an elephant. A huge table loomed over him like a mountain, a book rested on it, easily the size of a house. Scooter read the words on the front of the book.

Jam Inventions by Scooter McLay.

Wait.

He was still in the lab. It wasn't a different place, it was just that he was … *tiny.*

"Fizzbee?" Well at least his voice wasn't smaller. He still sounded exactly the same,

though perhaps a little shakier. Fizzbee's jam tart, easily the size of a dingy now, flew down towards him. She landed a short distance away, hopped out and toddled over. She was still slightly shorter than Scooter, but a lot rounder. Up close, her antennae were covered in tiny little suckers, her rubber-like skin glowing from inside.

"Is Scooter OK?" she asked a little nervously. "Does Scooter like this invention?"

"You invented a shrinking liquid?" Scooter looked all around him as Fizzbee nodded uncertainly. "Well now you've invented shrinking jam! Shrinking Strawberry." He paused. "Wait, do you have a growing liquid?"

"Yes, Scooter. Of course." Fizzbee dismissed the question.

"Phew." Scooter checked his hands, his legs, his feet. He touched his hair. It was still sticking up.

"So ... can I have a ride on your jam tart?"

He grinned. Fizzbee grinned back. She stretched
her antennae towards him and gently lifted him
onto the pastry rim. Scooter put his hand down
cautiously on the jam. It was firm, like sitting
on a bouncy castle.

Scooter frowned. He didn't feel safe. "What if
I fall out? Maybe we should make a seatbelt?"

"Scooter does not need to make a seatbelt."
Fizzbee shook her head as she stretched her
antennae out to the edges of the jam tart.

"But—" Scooter stopped as the light from

beneath her skin travelled slowly along her antennae, then continued towards him, surrounding him in a glowing blanket.

"Wow!" Scooter cried. "Is this a forcefield?"

"It is a Fizzbee seatbelt." Fizzbee nodded proudly. "Scooter will not fall. So, where shall Fizzbee fly?"

Scooter thought. "Why don't I show you what's outside?"

Fizzbee beamed at him, as the light pulsed once again and Scooter felt a thrill as the jam tart whizzed up towards the open window.

CHAPTER TEN

"Wooooo-hooooooo!" Scooter cried in delight as they zipped outside, waving to Gary as they passed him and soared up into the sky. The jam tart flew up and across the cloudless blue sky, zig-zagging and twisting and dancing.

123

"This is *amazing*!" Scooter laughed. "I can't believe how cool this—"

But he didn't get a chance to finish his sentence.

"Caaaaaaawwwwweeeeeee-ka-ka-ka."

A shadow passed overhead. Scooter looked up to see the greasy grey belly of a seagull hovering above, and shivered, despite the shining sun. It was huge! Its dark wings spread out like a giant feathery pterodactyl and, sitting in the tiny jam tart, Scooter suddenly felt more than a little vulnerable. He craned his neck to watch as the seagull's pink tongue poked out of its custard-coloured beak.

"I think that maybe we should get out of here." Scooter whispered as the seagull's black eyes focused on the jam tart. "*Quick!*" He shouted, pointing up to the seagull as its beady eyes opened wide with anticipation and it tucked its wings, ready to dive down towards them. "It's seen us!"

"It wants something, Scooter?" Fizzbee stared up as the bird dived towards them at increasing speed.

"Us! For dinner!" Scooter cried, not daring to take his eyes off the seagull, plunging towards them like an arrow shooting a target. "We need to get out of here!" He could almost see his reflection in its eyes. The seagull opened its dagger-like beak and...

"**Caaaaaaawwwwweeeeeeek.**"

It screeched in frustration as Fizzbee changed the direction of the jam tart.

"We not dinner!" She shouted at it, before flying away at full speed.

The seagull opened its wings, set its eyes on them

again and the chase began.

Fizzbee flew up. The seagull flew up.

Fizzbee flew down. The seagull flew down.

As she weaved the jam tart up and down and in and out, the seagull mimicked her every move, pecking at them and missing by millimetres each time.

Scooter desperately looked down towards the factory. If they could just make it back before the seagull reached them...

He turned to Fizzbee as she concentrated on ducking and weaving away from that beak, a bead of sweat on her brow, as the jam tart narrowly avoided being pecked once again.

They'd never make it back in time. Scooter turned towards the tower right beside them, the words *Dodgy Doughnuts* flickering from the top of it. One window was slightly ajar: big enough for a jam tart, but not for a seagull.

"Quick! In there!" He waved towards the window as Fizzbee changed direction. "It's not far. You can do it, Fizzbee!" Scooter held his breath as the seagull gained on them. It was so close. The smell of rotten fish from its last meal made his eyes water. The window wasn't far now, he could shoot jam balls further. But as Scooter turned back to the seagull, he froze as it opened its beak and he glimpsed the dark hole of its throat. He closed his eyes.

BANG.

The seagull splatted straight into the window, just as Fizzbee ducked the jam tart in through the small opening.

Scooter opened his eyes and turned back, just in time to watch the seagull slide slowly down the window.

"Ha!" He shouted. "Take that, Fish Breath!"

Fizzbee landed the jam tart on the window sill and sat down, panting.

"Are you all right?" Scooter asked.

"Not good, Scooter. Fizzbee does not like those things." She shook her head, breathlessly.

"No." Scooter sat down beside her. "That was a bit close. I never thought I'd say this but thank goodness for the Dodgy Doughnuts tower." He looked around. They were in an

office. It was empty and quiet. There was
a large wooden desk with a telescope on it.
Photos of a massive white guinea pig in a pink
ribbon lined every wall. Doughnut crumbs and
half-eaten Brussels sprouts littered a well-used
dog basket.

"That's weird." There were three sacks *full*
of Brussels sprouts in the corner of the room.
Not to mention all of the cardboard boxes
making some kind of tunnel. There was also a
whiteboard propped against the far wall, filled
with words and drawings and a map. Wait.
Was that a picture of a flying jam tart?

"Fizzbee!" Scooter gasped, his heart pounding again. "Daffy's planning to steal my jam inventions book and shut down our factory!" He read on. "She's been training her guinea pig to break in through the vents! Oh no…" His voice dropped to an urgent whisper. "She must have seen you flying into the vents!" He stared at the whiteboard in horror. "She's planning to release the wasps into the factory so that we have to make repairs and shut down, while she uses *our* jam recipes in *her* doughnuts!" Scooter read the final words on the whiteboard.

Tonight. Midnight.

"The robbery's tonight!" he cried. "We need to get back to the factory and make me full sized again right away! We've put the factory in terrible danger. It's time to tell my parents *everything*."

Fizzbee rummaged around inside her suitcase
before poking her head back out, her face
flustered as she scanned the desk nervously.

"Fizzbee is looking for the liquid that makes
the jam bubbles bigger." She scratched her
head. "Did Scooter move it?"

"No." Scooter shook his head. "It was right
there." He gestured towards the workbench

before his
eyes rested on
an empty bottle
lying on its side in
the plant pot below.
"You mean that one?"
He waved down to it.

"Yes!" Fizzbee nodded
before her face fell. "Oh."

"*That* was the growing solution?"
Scooter sat down heavily. "Do you have any
other growing solutions in there?" He nodded
towards her suitcase of bottles.

Fizzbee shook her head.

Scooter looked away for a moment, then
turned back to Fizzbee, his eyes fierce. "So,
just to clarify, I'm the height of a matchstick
with no way of getting back to my normal size
and a sneaky old woman and her evil guinea
pig are about to steal my inventions book and

sabotage our factory, all because they saw you flying around in a jam tart and realised they could break in through the vents?"

Fizzbee nodded again guiltily.

"Great." Scooter crossed his arms and turned away.

"Fizzbee didn't mean to make trouble." Fizzbee tried to apologise. "Sometimes Fizzbee can get excited."

"Yes." Scooter glared at her. "Just like when you messed around in the factory. Just like when you made me tiny, with *no way of reversing it*."

Tap tap.

There was a knock on the door.

"Is everything all right in there, Scoot?" Dad asked from outside the door. "Can I come in?"

"Um... Not right now, Dad." Scooter looked down at himself. How could he explain *this* to his parents? "I'm really busy with a new invention."

"You've been so busy over the last day or so." Dad pressed on. "We've hardly seen you." He paused. "Is this about having a pet? Because ... well,

your mum and I have been talking and I know you can't have a pet, but maybe you could have a friend over. Not just to the flat but, you know, to see the actual factory? Perhaps we've been a bit too cautious. If we told them the rules, then maybe…"

"It's fine, Dad." Scooter interrupted. He didn't think he wanted to hear whatever Dad was about to say. "I don't think we should let anyone new into the factory. They'll probably just *mess everything up*." Fizzbee's antennae drooped sadly.

"Do you want to come and have some pizza with us?" Dad asked hopefully and, actually, Scooter couldn't think of anything he'd rather do. But how could he explain his size? He was smaller than a slice of pepperoni!

"Thanks, Dad, but I'm going to carry on with this invention for now. I've got school tomorrow. I think I'll just have an early night."

"OK, Scoot. If you're sure. I'll leave a couple of slices in the fridge for you." Scooter listened to the sound of Dad's footsteps as he slowly walked away. He sat down on the workbench and put his head in his hands. His hair felt flat beneath his fingers.

How could he tell his parents that he'd lied to them? That he'd let an *alien* into their home? Worse, that he'd let an alien into the *factory*? He'd trusted Fizzbee and now he was going to be the size of a strawberry  for the rest of his life. And then there was the robbery...

"It's all my fault," he sighed. "I wanted you to stay. I didn't even notice that Daffy was watching us." His lemonade-bottle brain of ideas and determination felt empty and flat. "I just wanted..." He shrugged. "It doesn't matter."

"What does Scooter want?" Fizzbee asked gently.

"I wanted to show someone all the things that I can do." He shook his head. "We keep everything in the factory a secret. I've never been able to show any of my friends my inventions. I just wanted someone to see me." He glanced down at his left leg. *"All* of me."

"But, Scooter..." Fizzbee spoke gently. "Fizzbee *can* see you—"

"No." Scooter shook his head. "You don't understand—"

"Yes. Fizzbee understands." She interrupted him. "Fizzbee *can* see Scooter. *Fizzbee saw Scooter from space.*" She nodded her head firmly.

"What?" Scooter looked up. "What do you *mean*?"

She didn't answer right away. She looked at the floor for a moment, before turning to him.

"Fizzbee can see ideas." She smiled softly. "To me, they are colours." She lifted her little arm towards him. "They dance around your head, Scooter. Fizzbee has never seen colours like Scooter has. So bright. So ... beautiful." She opened her eyes wide, her antennae raising a little from her head. "Fizzbee saw the colours of your ideas from space and came here to see why a star was shining on Earth." She grinned. "But it was no star... It was Scooter." Her antennae stood boldly from her little head. "*Nobody* has colours like Scooter. *Nobody* has ideas like Scooter." She paused. "Fizzbee *loves* Scooter *because* Scooter is different. But..." She hung her head, her antennae drooping again. "If Scooter doesn't want Fizzbee to stay, then Fizzbee can go..."

"You can see ideas?" Scooter asked, unable

to hide his curiosity. "You see them as colours?" Fizzbee nodded. "So … what colours can you see around me now?"

"Brown." Fizzbee raised her eyebrows. "Like poo. Scooter has no ideas right now."

Scooter giggled. His hair stood a little straighter around his head.

"Ah." Fizzbee smiled. "Scooter is having an idea."

CHAPTER TWELVE

"The first thing we need to do is stop Daffy and Boris and the robbery." Scooter knelt on Hand-Bot One as it lifted him up to the whiteboard. He stood up carefully, using the Hand-Bot's thumb to steady himself, looked down and gave a small, determined nod. "We'll work out how to get me back to my normal size after that." Hand-Bot Two wrote a title on the whiteboard.

How to RUIN Daffy's Plan.
• Hide in Window.
SP

"We've got an advantage because we know their plan." Hand-Bot Two finished writing the title and waited, pen poised for Scooter to continue. "Daffy is going to use the hole in the window to sneak Boris into the factory's vents."

Hand-Bot Two drew a picture of a guinea pig in the vents. "Once he's found the Brussels battery and eaten the sprouts that power

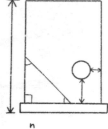

$$\sum_{i=1}^{n} (x_i - x)^2$$

the alarm, Daffy will break into the lab and take my jam inventions book." Hand-Bot Two began drawing a picture of Daffy by the window. "Then Boris will release the wasps into the factory as a distraction while the two of them make their escape." Hand-Bot Two began drawing wasps all

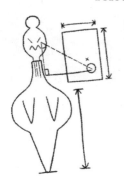

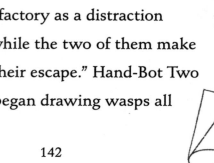

around the whiteboard. "But we're not going to let them release the wasps." Hand-Bot Two rubbed out the wasps. "If they got into the jam and the equipment, we'd have to shut the factory down until we could fix everything again."

Hand-Bot Two wrote the word 'factory' in large letters, then put a big cross dramatically through it.

"Not to mention that a wasp sting while I'm this size might even be fatal." Hand-Bot Two started drawing sad faces all around the whiteboard. "But we're not going to let that happen." Hand-Bot Two began wearily rubbing out the picture.

"I've got an idea. Obviously we could just fix the window. But I've got a feeling they'd still try and find a way in, especially now that they know about the vents. So, I say, we let them in. If we can get Daffy into the factory and stop Boris from releasing the wasps, then, with just a few adjustments, I think we can stop them from ever thinking about coming back here again." Scooter grinned. "If they want to see the factory, we'll show them the factory."

"Yeah! We show them!" Fizzbee cried.

The next few hours were spent in a flurry of activity as Scooter, Fizzbee and the Hand-Bots worked together to make the adjustments in preparation for Daffy and Boris.

Smoke billowed out of the lab as Scooter and the Hand-Bots soldered and welded and wired, while Fizzbee worked in the

factory drawing a target,
moving a large vat of jam to the centre
of the factory floor, detaching the seatbelts
from the roller-coaster cart and, finally,
helping Scooter and the Hand-Bots to screw
a giant new robotic tool to the ceiling of
the factory.

"I think that's everything." Scooter lifted
up the remote control they'd been making.
"I think we're ready."

"Yes." Fizzbee nodded. "This is Scooter's
factory." She punched her fist into the palm
of her hand with a devilish grin. "And we
will defend it."

Daffy put a small black sock over Boris' face. It had three holes cut into it, two for his eyes and one for his nose and mouth. "No one will recognise you now." She zipped up her brown tracksuit and picked up a jam jar.

"I've had another idea." She tapped the jar with her thin finger and placed it on the desk in front of Boris. She picked up a remote control and turned on the TV in the corner of the room. The screen filled with the sock-

covered face of a guinea pig burglar.

"Ha!" Daffy cried. "Aren't I clever? I've invented *Jam-Cam*! I'm going to leave it on a shelf in the jam inventions lab. They'll never know."

She grinned. "When they've finally fixed all of the damage we cause tonight, I'll still be one step ahead of them. I'll be able to copy every single invention those McLays come up with and they'll have no idea how to stop me." She picked up the Jam-Cam and put it carefully in her bag. "But one step at a time, eh, Boris?"

She picked him up and held him out in front of her.

"Ready?"

Boris nodded.

"OK." She lowered him carefully into her tool bag. "It's time."

Scooter knelt on Hand-Bot One as it reached down from the ceiling of the factory, then ran over the plan one last time with Fizzbee. He checked his watch: **11.59pm**. Any second now and they'd be here.

"You know what to do?" He checked again.

"Yes." Fizzbee nodded. "Fizzbee will get Daffy onto the roller coaster. Fizzbee knows what to do."

"OK." Scooter smiled. "Good luck. You'd better get back to the lab. I'll see you soon."

He watched as Fizzbee zipped towards the vents, her chin set in determination. He clutched the remote control … and waited.

CHAPTER THIRTEEN

Daffy stood at the front window of the jam
factory, peering in through the small round hole.

Everything seemed quiet.

"It's all clear, Boris." She opened up her tool
bag and pulled out an extendable screwdriver.
She pushed it carefully through the hole in the
window, being careful not to touch the glass

and extended it towards the vent. Slowly, she unwound the screws on each corner of the vent panel, then took out a long piece of piping and pushed it through the hole in the window and into the vent, creating a perfect tunnel for Boris to crawl into. She picked Boris up, holding him in front of her face.

"You know what you're doing?" He nodded. "You can have as much of your special chocolate sauce as you like at the end of this job. Minus the sprouts." Boris nodded again. "Good luck."

She kissed him gently on the nose, lifted him into the pipe and listened to his scurrying footsteps as he scrambled towards the vent. "I'll meet you in the jam inventions lab."

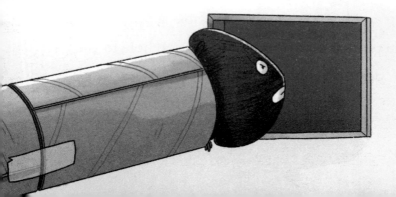

Fizzbee was waiting. Any moment now and the red light of the alarm would switch off. That's when Daffy would be coming in to take the inventions book. Fizzbee flexed her antennae. All she needed to do was to get Daffy onto the roller coaster – and she knew exactly how she was going to do it...

Scooter watched as Boris climbed out of the vent. Was he wearing a *sock* on his head? He looked like a little bandit! Boris sniffed the air cautiously, then jumped onto a conveyor belt next to a line of jam jars. He let the conveyor

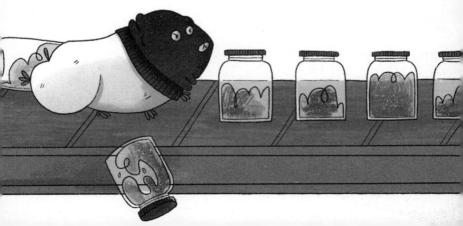

belt carry him for a short while before hopping off it and onto the Blueberry Burst pipe. Then, like a tightrope walker, he tiptoed across it.

He'd been well trained. Scooter couldn't help feeling impressed. He watched as Boris sprang down from the Blueberry Burst pipe to the floor and made his way confidently to the Brussels battery. Scooter looked at his watch. It would probably take at least half an hour for Boris to get through the sprouts that powered the alarm. Maybe he should sit down for a minute and...

His mouth fell open as Boris started chowing down the sprouts like a pneumatic drill through concrete. At that rate, it would only take a minute or two.

SCOOTER'S
EXTRA-POWERFUL
LONG-LASTING
BRUSSELS SPROUT
POWERED BATTERY

Any second now and Daffy would be
climbing in through the window of the lab.

Scooter's hand hovered over the remote
control.

Any ... second ... now.

Daffy watched as the light on
the window alarm went off,
and smiled. Boris had done
his work perfectly. Now he
just needed to release the
wasps and they could
head home together
safe in the knowledge
that McLay's Jam was
finished. She took a
crowbar out of her bag,
levered open the window
and climbed inside.

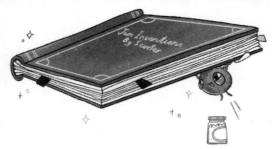

Fizzbee watched as Daffy squeezed herself awkwardly through the lab window. She stood up and brushed herself down. Then she took something out of her bag and crammed it in among the jars of jam before turning towards the jam inventions book with a grin.

It was time.

Fizzbee stretched out her antennae to either side of the book and lifted it up.

Boris was pleased with himself. He'd made it through the vents, onto the conveyor belt, over the pipe and down to the Brussels battery. He looked at the carnage of sprouts on the floor and smiled.

Daffy would be proud.

All he had to do now was release the wasps.

"Squee–ee–eee–eee–eee–ee–eeaak."

That was Boris's most evil squeak. He'd been practising it for this exact moment. He rubbed his paws together and turned to look at the wasp testing area.

Wait … *what was that?*

Daffy watched in utter confusion as the jam inventions book lifted from the table and flew out through the steel door. Flying jam tarts were one thing … but flying *books*? What on earth was going on? Books didn't fly. She followed it out of the lab into the factory reception and watched as it floated towards the roller-coaster cart. Daffy had never been on a roller coaster before. Would there be time for a quick ride, she wondered? No. She had to get that book and get out of here.

She reached forwards. The book floated backwards. She took a step onto the cart and

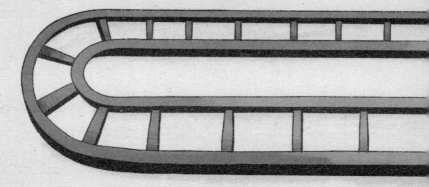

reached for it again. It floated back a little
further. Finally, she put her whole weight onto
the roller-coaster cart, but before she had a
chance to reach for the book again, the cart
powered up, the factory doors swung open and
Daffy found herself propelled
backwards onto the seat.

CHAPTER FOURTEEN

Scooter watched as the giant robotic bubble wand hovered above Boris.

"You're not going one step further." He pressed a button on his remote control and the robotic hairdryer blew a small puff of air into the bubble wand.

One solitary bubble grew out of it, jiggling and joggling until it was a perfectly round and beautiful jam bubble. The robotic bubble wand gently shook it free.

Boris watched, spellbound, as a large rainbow-coloured bubble floated towards him, shimmering and sparkling above. His eyes crossed, still watching as the bubble touched his nose.

"Squeeeaak?"

Wait a minute. What was going on? The bubble didn't pop. In fact, it was slowly sinking over him until he was ... inside it.

"Squeeeaak!"

He scurried forwards. This wasn't part of the plan. He'd better get out of this trap, pronto. But instead of bursting, the bubble simply began to roll forwards, before gently lifting into the air, Boris still inside it.

"Squeeeeaaaaaakkkk!"

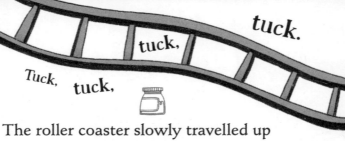

Tuck, tuck, tuck, tuck.

The roller coaster slowly travelled up towards the roof of the factory as Daffy sat inside. She checked behind her for the flying book, but the factory doors had closed and she was too high to jump out now. Oh well, she thought as she sat back. She'd wanted a ride on this roller coaster since the moment she saw it. Might as well enjoy it now. But, as she travelled upwards, she heard a squeak.

"Boris?" The cart hung in mid-air at the very top of the factory, a huge drop below her.

"Squuueeeeeeaaakkkkk."

Daffy gasped. A disgruntled-looking Boris was floating up towards her. He appeared to be stuck inside a large bubble. The roller coaster would go right past him. If she could just…

"I'm coming!"

Whoosh!

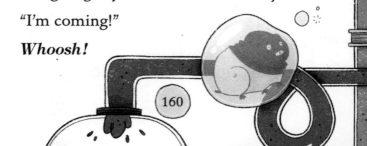

"...BORRRRRRIIIIIIIIISSSSSSSSSSSSSSSSSSS."

The roller coaster flew down towards
the factory floor, Daffy clinging on from
inside the cart, her eyes opened wide and her
bun streaming loose behind her, the biggest
grin of excitement on her face.

"*Wheeeeeeeeeeeeeeee!*"

The roller coaster looped around.

"*Heeeeeeeeeeeeeeee!*"

It took a sharp turn, buffeting her to the
side. Oh, it was wonderful! It whizzed up
another hill and Daffy saw Boris, his front
legs scurrying forwards as the bubble floated
towards her. She leant forwards, grabbed it
with both hands and pulled him onto her lap.

"It's all fine, Boris. I'm right here." She patted the bubble affectionately, before frowning and lifting one of her hands. It was sticky. She gave it a cautious sniff. "It's jam, Boris! You can eat your way out! Eat the bubble." She looked ahead. "There's a loop the loop coming up!" She grinned gleefully. "We're going to go upside down!" She held her breath in anticipation as the roller-coaster cart sped down another hill, up around the loop and ... stopped.

For a moment Daffy and Boris hung upside down in the roller-coaster cart.

Then they fell head first into a vat of jam below.

Fizzbee returned the jam inventions book to the lab, then whizzed through the vents to join Scooter.

"It's all going perfectly." He smiled at her. "Look! They've just fallen into the jam vat, right on target." He pressed the next button on the remote control.

Daffy clambered out of the vat. She was covered from head to toe in Cherry Candy Floss Jam, but for some reason, and this was a very new experience for Daffy, she was giggling. Not just giggling, it was more than that. She was brimming with ... what was it?

Excitement?

Joy?

Wind?

She wriggled. No. It was definitely a *feeling*. Something had happened on that roller-coaster ride. Something weird. All of a sudden, she didn't want to sabotage the factory. In fact, all she could think about was having another ride on that roller coaster.

"Oh, cheer up, Boris." She lifted Boris, still inside the jam bubble, and licked

some jam off her lips. "You must admit, that was a little bit fun." Her smile dropped. "Seems a shame to wreck it, really." She watched a giant robotic hair dryer position itself in front of them, then blast them with warm air.

For a moment, she enjoyed the warm breeze in her face. That was, until her face started to dry and harden and tighten and actually, she had a little itch on her nose that she needed to scratch. But as she went to lift her arm, it wouldn't budge. She tried again, a little harder this time. Nope. She couldn't move her arms or her legs. It must have been the hairdryer. The heat had

turned the jam solid like a boiled sweet around her, encasing her inside. She rolled her eyes, the only part of her body that she could still move, then looked at Boris, his bubble stuck firmly to her hands.

"There's something funny going on here, Boris." She spoke through fixed lips, looking sideways at the huge robotic tools. "It's like the factory's alive or something. And it's rumbled us. We'd better get out of here."

"Squeeak." Boris agreed.

"Come on, then. Eat your way out of there, then eat me free and let's scarper."

Boris nodded. Things hadn't gone quite to

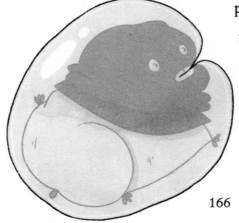

plan: it was time to leave.

He opened his mouth and began to eat his way out of the bubble.

"Yes!" Fizzbee and Scooter high fived. "That worked perfectly!" Scooter grinned. "They're not going anywhere. Let's replace the sprouts that Boris ate, then the alarm will go off and the police will come and take them away." He stepped off the Hand-Bot and into the jam tart with Fizzbee.

They hovered up and past Daffy, who was standing like a statue as Boris gnawed at the bubble in her hands.

CRACK!

"What was that?" Scooter turned back.

It seemed to come from Daffy and Boris but...

What was it?

CREAK!

Boris' bubble began to shatter like a pane of broken glass.

"What's happening?" Scooter frowned.

They stared as white fur poked out from the bubble, like a gigantic chick hatching from an egg. And what on earth was going on with Boris? Was he ... *getting bigger?*

"The edible jam bubbles!" Scooter exclaimed. "You added a drop of growing solution to the mix before the bottle fell.

We never actually ate one, did we?" He stared down at Boris. "He's eating the bubble! It's making him *grow*!" Boris was easily the size of a rather large chicken now, his bottom squarely in Daffy's horrified frozen face.

And he was *still* growing.

"We need to get the Shrinking Strawberry Jam." Scooter whispered urgently, not daring to take his eyes off the bulging guinea pig as the jam bubble shattered entirely, knocking Daffy to the floor like a skittle.

"What's happening, Boris?" She tried to wriggle free, Boris now growing at a steady rate beside her. The flying jam tart hovered above and her eyes opened wide as she saw the

McLay boy sitting inside it, except he was tiny. And beside him was ... *what was that?* It looked like a little orange rubber ball ... except it had arms and legs and eyes and antennae and ... oh my giddy aunt, it was an *alien*! A little, orange and very round alien!

This was getting a bit too weird now.

Time to get out of here.

But Daffy couldn't move, and something very strange was happening to Boris. Any second now and he'd be the size of a small hippopotamus. The boy turned to look at her, his eyes wild.

"Help him!" she called desperately. "Help my little Boris!"

CHAPTER FIFTEEN

"SQQQUUUUUUEEEEEAAAAAKKKKK!"

Boris let out a high-pitched squeak of irritation.

cRACK!

He knocked the glass wall of the wasp testing area.

CR-AAAA-AAAA-AAAAAA-AAAAAAAA-CK

A zigzag of cracks began to work their way through the glass.

"We've got to stop him!" Scooter turned to Fizzbee. "He'll wreck the factory if he keeps growing like this. Not

171

to mention what will happen if the wasps get out! You'll have to get the Shrinking Strawberry Jam while I try and keep the wasp wall in one piece." Scooter clambered onto Hand-Bot One and pushed a series of buttons on the remote control, ordering his inventions to work. He turned to Fizzbee, still hovering uncertainly in her jam tart. "Go!" he shouted. "It's up to you now!"

Fizzbee flew with lightning speed through the vents to the jam inventions lab and over to the vat of Shrinking Strawberry Jam. She searched desperately for a spoon or something big enough to carry the jam in.

"SQUUUUEEEEEAAAAAAKKKKK," Boris echoed down the vents.

There wasn't a second to waste. With no time to think, Fizzbee dunked her jam tart into the vat of Shrinking Strawberry Jam, lifted it unsteadily and carried it like a bowl towards the vent. But wait! There was one more thing she'd need. With every ounce of speed left in her, she zipped back into the lab, dipped her hand into the jar of Cherry Candy Floss Jam, then flew back to the factory as fast as she could manage.

"SQUUUUEEEEEAAAAAAKKKKK."

Boris was annoyed.

This whole break-in was a total bust.

Even after all of the training and tasting and tightrope walking, he'd been captured by a jam bubble, taken for a ride on a roller coaster, dunked in a vat of jam and now he was being made *bigger*? He looked down at Daffy far below, just as a light glinted on the sparkly *Best Friends* pendant around her neck.

Best friends? Some best friend. He didn't even *like* jam! But had she asked him that? No! She was far too busy trying to take over the world! Or, the jam world, at least.

Well, he'd show her! He'd show them all!

Daffy and the McLays were about to find out *exactly* what Boris thought of jam.

"Boris?" Daffy wriggled her way out of her jam encasing and looked up. Boris was the size of an elephant! She followed his gaze down to the pendant around her neck, then slowly back up towards his face.

"Oh no, Boris!" She backed away. She knew that look. "Don't do it!"

Boris strained.

"He's gonna *blow*!" she cried.

Under Scooter's orders, the paintbrush, hairdryer and now also the robotic hands filled the cracks with jam, pastry, jam balls … *anything* to keep the wasps inside.

He risked a peek at Boris and gasped. He was huge! And he was *about to do a gigantic poo in the factory*!

Fizzbee raced forwards, sweat dripping down her brow as she wove in and out through the factory equipment, flying her jam tart towards a gigantic squeaking, straining Boris.

There was only one way to get the shrinking jam into him.

She flew above his face, hovered as he looked up at her, released her antennae and dropped her jam tart straight into his mouth.

"Fizzbee?" Scooter watched
as Fizzbee released her jam tart
into Boris' open mouth below.
For a moment she hung in mid-air
and then, like a stone, she fell.

"Fizzbee! Noooooooooooooo!"
He desperately tapped his remote control.
"Quickly!" He shouted. "We have to catch her!"
But as Hand-Bot One whizzed towards her,
Scooter could already see that it was too late.
His eyes met with hers as she dropped, her
hand lifting to her mouth. "Fizz..."

POP.

Scooter blinked.

Fizzbee's little round body
quadrupled in size and puffed up like
an inflated balloon.

"Sorry, Scooter. Fizzbee broke
the rules." She waved sheepishly.

"Fizzbee ate Cherry Candy Floss Jam!" She waved as she floated up towards the ceiling.

"SQQUUUUUEE..."

The jam tart fell into Boris' open mouth.

GULP.

"...eeeeaaaaaaakkkkkkk."

Like the air escaping a balloon, Boris deflated.

"Squeak."

He piped up at them, still annoyed.

"Phew." Scooter breathed a sigh of relief. "That didn't go exactly as..." He didn't get a chance to finish his sentence.

Mum and Dad stood at the factory doors, their faces drained of colour, their eyes blinking rapidly as they took in the scene in front of them. Crystallized jam all over the floor … cracks all through the glass of the wasp testing area … a giant bubble wand … and … Daffy Dodgy? And her guinea pig too?

"What's all this?" Scooter's mum stepped forwards.

"Come on, Boris." Daffy interrupted. It was time to leave. And sharpish. She pulled Boris tight towards her and couldn't help noticing

that he felt just a tad smaller than before. She stroked his soft white fur and held him up to her face. "Do you even like jam, Boris?"

The little guinea pig shook his head sharply.

"I've gone off it a bit myself." She kissed his nose. "Come on. Let's go." She glared at Scooter's mum and dad. *"And we're never coming back."* She stormed past them, before climbing out of the window. "I think it's time we had a holiday," they heard her mutter as she stalked back to Dodgy Doughnuts. "I don't think I'd mind if I never see another speck of jam in my life."

"Squeeeaaak." Boris agreed.

Scooter's parents watched her leave, utterly bemused.

"It's OK, Mum and Dad." Hand-Bot One lifted Scooter in front of their faces.

"Scooter?" Dad spluttered. "Wh-what happened? Why are you so *small*? And…" He looked at Fizzbee, still puffed up like a balloon. "What's *that*?"

"Don't worry." Scooter smiled reassuringly. "Everything's going to be fine."

Mum and Dad both nodded, dumbstruck.

Pop. Fizzbee resumed her normal size, hopped in a jam tart and flew up towards them.

"Yes. All OK." She grinned impishly as Dad fainted into Mum's arms.

One Month Later...

Scooter watched as the '**FOR SALE**' sign went up outside the factory.

"We'll find another place, son." Dad put his hand on Scooter's shoulder.

"I don't want another place," Scooter sighed.
"I like it here." Fizzbee hovered beside his
shoulder in a jam tart. "Fizzbee likes it here
too." She nodded her little orange head, her
eyes sad.

"We've outgrown it, Scoot, we don't have
the space for all of your wonderful inventions.
Especially since…" Mum glanced warily
towards Fizzbee. She still wasn't quite used to
the idea of an alien living with them.

It hadn't been easy convincing them to let Fizzbee stay. But in Scooter's typically determined way, he'd refused to take no for an answer.

As soon as he was back to normal size (after eating an edible jam bubble) he had spent night and day telling them all about how Fizzbee had in fact saved his life *and* saved their factory, while putting her own life at risk. In the end, they had wearily agreed but only on the express understanding that Scooter would *never* hide something like that from them again. Plus, all Shrinking Strawberry Jam had to be kept under lock and key and Fizzbee's suitcase of bottles and inventions had to be put back in her spaceship.

Earth wasn't ready for those inventions just yet.

In the month since the break-in, nobody had heard from Daffy or Boris, and Scooter wondered, not for the first time, where they'd gone to. Dodgy Doughnuts had been boarded up with a sign on the front stating that anyone who wanted doughnuts could bog off.

The postman walked up the path towards them, stopping for a moment to take in the '**FOR SALE**' sign. He handed an envelope to Scooter with a smile.

Scooter inspected it. Written in messy, scrawling handwriting were the words:

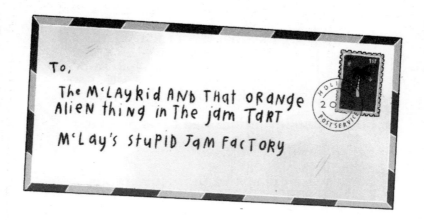

He opened it.

Inside was a postcard.

We Definitely don't WISH YOU WERE HERE

Beneath was a picture of Daffy and Boris smiling beside a huge roller coaster. Boris was holding a doughnut covered in his favourite guinea-pig-friendly chocolate sauce. Daffy had dyed her hair pink. They were both wearing a pink sparkly heart-shaped *Best Friends* pendant.

On the back of the postcard was a rough scrawl.

HeRE ARE the keys To my ~~stinking~~ FacTory. It's ~~your problem~~ yours Now. Boris and I have DEcided to TraVEL The WORLD. Your FactoRy is BETTer than MINE Anyway so you might as weLL ~~do it up for us while we enjoy ourselves~~ Have it. I hope That COVERS any damAge.

BEST wisHes,
DaffY and BORIS

Fizzbee hovered by Scooter's shoulder as he read the note, a little frown filling her face. Seeing that picture of Daffy and Boris reminded her of something that she'd been meaning to tell Scooter. Something from that night they broke in.

"Scooter..." She began. But she never finished her sentence.

"We can stay after all!" Scooter interrupted, as he looked down at a key inside the envelope, smiling from ear to ear as he handed the note to his parents.

"We might need something a bit more formal than this." Mum mused as she read it.

"And there's a lot of work to do over in that factory." Dad chipped in.

"But it would be big enough." Scooter watched as Dad pulled out the 'FOR SALE' sign. "Big enough for some *new* inventions…" He turned to Fizzbee, grinning broadly. "Don't you think?"

"Yes." She nodded, that *something* forgotten for now, her eyes bright with happiness as she lifted her little arm towards his head. "I see that Scooter is already having ideas."

"Yep." Scooter pulled out a folded picture of a quad bike from his pocket. "Here's what I've been thinking…"

And so, as Scooter and Fizzbee planned, and Daffy and Boris partied, Gary the snail was … well… Gary was peeking through the window.

Because Gary had noticed that very something that Fizzbee had just forgotten about.

It was a something that was inside the jam inventions lab. A something that he didn't think ought to be there.

In fact, if Scooter and Fizzbee had gone into the jam inventions lab at that precise moment, then they might have noticed that something too.

Nestled among the shelves of jam, a little red light blinked out from one of the jam jars. The little red light of a hidden Jam-Cam…

But that's another story.

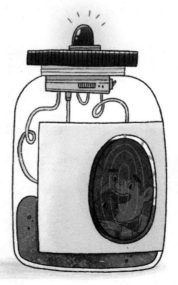

The End

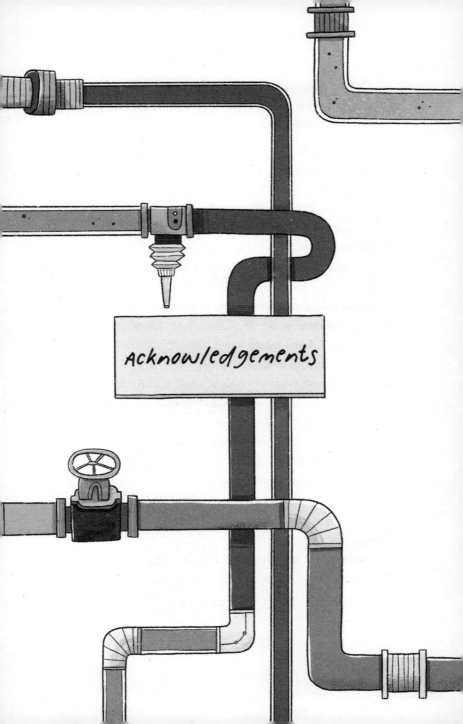
Acknowledgements

Writing a book is like inventing a new flavour of jam. You need a dash of inventiveness, a pinch of humour and lots of special ingredients – or in this case, special people.

Thank you so much to:

- Agent of awesomeness, Kate Shaw.
- My Editors, Non Pratt and Frances Taffinder; Designer, Jamie Hammond; and everyone at Walker Books. Loveliest. Team. *Ever*.
- Jenny Taylor – for taking the pictures from my head and putting a better version into the pages of our book.
- Emma Greenwood, Imogen Cooper and the team at The Golden Egg Academy. I wouldn't be here without you.
- My amazing writer buddies; Kate, Elizabeth, George, Cathie, Adam, John, Kerry, Georgia, Sarah, Amy, Alex & Jenny. #Moraleishigh.
- My brilliant family – Mum, Dad, Colin, Anne, Matt, Helen, Thomas, Isaac, Jona, Marie-Lou, Evie, Oliver, Dave, Stacey, Faithe & Jax.
- All of my lovely friends and especially Smallie, Joshie, Lucy, Rob, Albert, Edith, Michelle, Lindsay & Laura.
- Abigail, my goddaughter, whose enormous sense of fun and incredible determination inspired Scooter. And her mum, Carrie, for the invaluable guidance and friendship.
- And finally, my wonderful husband, Richie and our two children, Meg and Hattie, for always believing in me (and most of the funny bits).